CATENAE

by

S E Curtis

Catenae

S E Curtis

Lulu Edition

If you like this story, please contact me at
SECurtisTX@yahoo.com

Printed in the United States of America

First Printing, 2013

ISBN: 978-1-312-21367-8

Cover image courtesy of fotographic1980 at
FreeDigitalPhotos.net

Table of Contents

Catena 1: Tamara

Catena 2: Danny

Catena 3: Tamara Prime

Catena 4: Lerys

Catena 5: Alea

Catena 6: Kyren

Catena 7: Lao Ran Jun

Catena 1

Tamara's world flipped inside out with a flash of blue-white light and she stood again at the top of the stairs, six seconds in the past. Her senses reeled as she fought to refocus. Her failsafe had triggered, meaning she had died.

The assassin had been waiting behind the lion's perch at the bottom of the library stairs.

Tamara dashed to her left, drawing her flechette gun, and circled behind the lion, but the killer wasn't there.

He wrapped his arm around her neck to jerk her chin up, and cut her throat. She collapsed in a shower of arterial spray.

Tamara's world flipped with another flash and she was back on the landing, again six seconds earlier. She staggered, nearly falling down the stairs as she drew her pistol. She let her momentum carry her down the last few steps. Again the killer wasn't there. She let herself fall to the flagstone sidewalk, avoiding his first attack. She tumbled away, evading his slash instinctively. She rolled to her feet and blocked his next slash, but her arm cracked audibly under the force of his immense strength, and she gasped.

His yellow eyes glittered, and the nails of his hands were long, curved claws. A Shen Tiger Soldier! How was that possible?

Tamara triggered her d 'Alembert field. Her world flipped again and she was in her apartment. She fell to her knees. Consecutive *peregrinations* wreaked havoc on the conscious mind.

Something catastrophic must have happened for the Family to let the Shen reach fruition and gain enough confidence to openly attack.

Tamara grabbed the backpack she had stashed away just for this kind of emergency bug-out. Someone was out to kill her, and he was a time traveler. And that meant she had to find him and kill him first.

Suddenly he was there in her apartment. Shit! She shot at his legs and he fell as she climbed out to the rusted iron fire escape. She was halfway down when he leaned out over the railing. She crashed through the nearest window as needles plinked like hail off the stairs. One of the darts ricocheted in the right direction and pierced her calf. Glass slashed her hands and arms as she landed in the screaming neighbor's living room. Abruptly there was too much blood around and none of it someone else's.

Tamara tried to roll to her feet, but her leg wouldn't support her. The denim of her jeans turned dark and shiny wet as she watched. She ignored the screaming woman, the blood, and the pain, and invoked a destination she had prepared for just such a situation.

The world turned inside-out. Her mind groaned under the fourth *peregrination* in, what, twenty seconds? If she tried that too many more times, she would shut down.

Then it was a year earlier, a hot, humid night in Texas. She lay in a dark corner just outside an emergency room. She thrust the gun into her backpack and crawled into the light, leaving a trail of blood. Someone shouted.

"Get a stretcher!"

"What is it?"

"A girl. Bleedin' all over the place."

Activity bustled around her as they gave her first aid, decided her wounds were not fatal, and rolled her into the hospital. She let herself relax. Humans could be horrible to one another, but they also had an impulse to compassion that she had learned to trust.

It's why she spent so much time here, on the homeworld of her ancestors.

Catena 2

"Doctor Nolan! Her heart rate is still slowing."

"Dammit!" A moment of baffled panic shook me. She wasn't that seriously injured! "The atropine is in?"

"Atropine is in," answered the nurse across the bed.

"Down to thirty-four bpm. A-Fib!" The technician monitoring the EKG called out. It began to beep an alarm but he thumbed it off. "RVR!"

A quiet coldness filled me, as it always did when I realized death had come again to throw the dice. My nascent panic ceased, and the sense of rattled uncertainty disappeared in the need to face down a crisis.

She wasn't presenting any other symptoms yet. She'd fallen unconscious, but all she had were lacerations and a perfect, tiny hole through her leg, a wound I could not explain. Her chest was starting to rise and fall more rapidly. I placed my stethoscope on her chest. Her lungs were clear. Her heartbeat was still slowing, though. Then I heard it. A skip in the rhythm. A moment later the technician frowned at his readout.

There it was again. "PVC," I said. The tech nodded without looking up. I began to count the number of beats between the regular beats and the skip, a premature ventricular contraction. Something was doing a number on her heart. It had to be a toxin. But the blood work hadn't come back yet. Then the skips began to repeat without returning to the regular beat, a series of three or four cycles before it returned to normal.

Oh hell.

"VT," said the tech. "Not sustained." He continued to watch the beats I listened to.

I said to the nurse, "Call Doctor Varma. She's going to crash."

The nurse hesitated a moment.

"Now!" I snapped. "I'm calling the code."

The nurse plugged her jack into the com system in the wall behind the patient and issued the instructions.

In answer, the intercom thunked to life. "Code Blue!" said the voice of the unit secretary. "ER three."

Exclamations sounded out in the hallway, and an assistant peeked in curiously.

"Thirty BPM and falling," said the EKG tech.

Shit. Her heart rate was still falling even while the ventricles tried to increase the pace. Her heart was beating at two different paces now, which meant it was only a matter of time before--

"V-Fib!" the technician called. Another alarm cried from his monitor.

"Bag her!" I said to the nurse. I pressed the heels of my hands to her chest and began CPR as the nurse fitted a silicone mask over her face and began to compress the attached balloon.

Then the crash team was there with the cart and applying electrodes to her chest. The defibrillator began to beep, registering the rhythms and arrhythmia of her heart. It also began a high-pitched whine as it built up its charge. A light on it turned red and the monitoring tech said:

"Clear!"

The nurse and I took our hands away. The machine clicked and the patient jerked at the jolt. The defibrillator analyzed the results of the shock, then decided a second shock was necessary. The woman jerked again. A light on the machine flashed amber.

"Epinephrine," I said. "Two units. And get me the BMP results!"

"BP Sixty-over-thirty and falling", said the second nurse.

The patient jerked as the defibrillator delivered a third shock.

"Come on!" I growled, glaring at the readout.

"Three hundred milligrams amiodarone in five-DW," said a new, firm voice as the attending physician entered the room.

"No!" I said without thinking. The startled glances the others gave me for contradicting the grizzled AP was the equivalent of stunned gasps. Dr. Varma cocked a bushy, salt-and-pepper brow at me.

"Doctor Nolan?"

"I think it's a toxin, sir," I said. "Cardenolide."

"The BMP shows hypokalemia?"

"The panel hasn't come back yet."

Dr. Varma stared at the EKG readout. "Yes," he said. "I see the U-wave and the flattened T. Have you ruled out hypercalcemia or hyperthyroidism?"

"No sir," I said. A year ago I would have felt unsure of myself and chagrined. But not now.

"The source?"

"A puncture wound in her leg."

"Hmmm," Varma said, studying the patient's chart. Finally he said, "I concur with Doctor Nolan. DigiFab, four hundred milligrams."

The defibrillator was removed and the antitoxin administered. The fall of her heart rate and blood pressure stopped almost immediately and she began to stabilize.

The older man said, "Don't forget the extra paperwork for the police."

I nodded. The toxin turned this from a freak accident into a potential attempted homicide.

A nurse brought Doctor Varma a clipboard. He glanced at it and handed it to me. The blood panel results. It showed acute hypokalemia. "Good call, Danny." He slapped me on the arm and left.

I moved out of the way of the others as they worked on the woman. I gazed at her, dark hair, smooth, dusky skin, wondered why someone would try to kill her.

She had appeared outside the door of the E.R. as if out of thin air. No trace of blood trail leading up to that spot, and no sign of a mugging anywhere around the area. I checked her leg wound. It was perfectly circular, through and through, and smaller than any caliber of bullet I knew of. I'd need an x-ray to verify, but I suspected there would be an equally perfect hole through her tibia as well. But it wasn't a gunshot wound. There was no evidence of impact trauma, no marginal abrasion or lacerations. Just a three millimeter hole.

If it had been made with a projectile, it had to have been some kind of nail gun.

"Let's clean and debride her wounds," I said. "I'll be back later to suture 'em. If the wound on her leg looks good, we'll put a cast on." I turned to leave and caught sight of her backpack sitting in the corner. I picked it up and carried it out to the nurses' station. "Any id on her yet, Jules?" The secretary shook her head. "Here's her pack. Let's see if we can find some." The pack contained clothes, a pair of running shoes, and, interestingly, a tool kit. I'd half expected a bag of school books.

"What in the world?" the secretary said. She pulled what looked like a gun from the pack. Well, it almost looked like a gun. I took it from her and turned it over. It was light and small. But its barrel was diamond shaped, not round, and too small to shoot anything except maybe BBs.

"A toy," I muttered. It felt as light as plastic, but it wasn't plastic. It wasn't metal either. But it was incredibly hard and scratch resistant. And the trigger wouldn't budge, not even a little, as if it were welded in place. No markings. No serial number. No toy company logo.

"Ah!" said the secretary. She pulled a card from the pack, scanned it, and handed it to me with a pleased smile.

It was a New York driver's license with the woman's face with a slight smile. "Tamara Decaire". It had a Manhattan zip code. "You're a long way from home." Age twenty-five. No medical alerts. I handed it back. "Okay, put her in the system. And find any next-of-kin information.

Don't call 'em yet. It's two a.m. and she's stable, so we can wait til morning."

"Yes, Doctor."

A shout and crash rang out behind me. The patient, Tamara, staggered out of the room. She'd torn her gown off and the IV tube out of her arm. She saw me and shouted "What did you do to me!" She had a faint, unrecognizable accent. Not a New York accent.

I held out my hand and approached her. "It's okay. You're safe, Tamara. How can I help you?"

The woman's eyes narrowed as she stared at me. Then she saw her backpack behind me on the desk. She charged toward it, but her disorientation made her stagger. She fell into me. I caught her as she sagged. Then she was limp in my arms, unconscious again. I picked her up like a child. Ugh. She was heavier than she looked. I carried her back to the room. Both nurses lay on the floor. I paused a moment to gape at them. I placed her back on the bed, then checked my comrades. They were both fine, just knocked unconscious. They said she'd awakened and moved with startling speed, and judo or karate-chopped them into senselessness. I stared at the patient. That little girl had done that?

I ordered a sedative added to her treatment—along with fluids and antibiotics—not too much of one, but enough to keep her out while we took care of her. I looked in on her from time to time between my other duties. She perplexed me. Toward sunrise I sutured her wounds, including the one in her leg. An x-ray had shown me that the hole had indeed perfectly perforated her tibia as well, so I ordered a cast. Then I authorized her move to the ICU.

My shift ended at noon. I had twelve hours to kill before I had to be back at the hospital. As I walked out of the sliding front doors, I felt the letdown that always accompanied my departure from the hospital. I put my helmet on and climbed on my bike. It came to life with a throaty roar and I raced out of the parking lot. I wasn't in a hurry to get home. I just lost myself in the speed and agility of the bike. I never rode straight home. I preferred taking a scenic route through some wooded neighborhoods with lots of curves and few stop signs. I wasn't thinking about the scenery though.

When I got to my apartment I changed into shorts and a t-shirt and went to the gym and spent an hour working myself to sweaty exhaustion. I returned home and took a long, cold shower. Finally I went into the kitchen, poured myself a generous gin and tonic, and sank into my recliner.

I sat on something hard and reached for it. It was the toy gun with the small, diamond-shaped barrel. I stared at it. I must have slipped it into my pocket when the secretary handed me Tamara's driver's license. I turned it over in my hand, then set it on the side table.

I finished the drink, made another. Made a third. I should not have, but I got up, walked slowly back to the kitchen, and made a fourth. I returned to the recliner, sagged into it, raised the glass to the empty room, and drained it.

I slept and didn't remember my dreams.

I never slept long. I was lucky in that I only needed four or five hours of sleep and I was recharged. I went back in to the hospital about four hours early. I walked the halls of the maternity ward, pausing to visit with the nurses and look at the newborns. Obstetrics would have been my specialty had I not been swayed by the immediacy and importance of emergency medicine.

Then I went to visit Tamara. She was in the ICU now, her arms bandaged, her leg in a cast. I checked her chart, then cancelled the sedative. They would last through the night, and she'd be awake and able to answer questions in the morning.

Catena 1

When Tamara woke, things weren't right. She sat up fast, pulling half a dozen tubes and cords around her.

"Whoa!" The doctor caught the teetering IV hanger as beeps began to sound behind her. He reached toward her and she recoiled. He deliberately slowed his motion. "It's okay." He reached behind her to reset the alarm.

Tamara wasn't listening to him. She focused inward, gaping at the blank emptiness in her head. She was groggy, and nauseated, and close to outright panic. Her *ai* was gone, and with it her knowledge and her ability to *peregrinate*.

Relax. Calm down. Breathe. It can't be gone. These people lack the capability to even recognize it, much less remove it. So, damaged? Okay. How long would it take the nanites to repair it?

She tried to speak, but her voice was hoarse and thready.

"I'm hungry," she whispered. Food. The nanites used her metabolic energy as their power source.

"Lunch'll be served in about two hours," the doctor said.

"Now." Tamara used the most forceful whisper she could.

She finally looked at him. He was young, and had startlingly blue eyes. For a moment, she gazed at his face, her intentions forgotten.

He said something, but she didn't hear him. Under different circumstances...

He glanced at the file in his hand and said her real name, "Tamara Decaire."

She snapped back to reality. She didn't use a false name. No need to. She was a thousand years and a hundred light years removed from her home. Now, though, her name was in the hospital's system; now she was casting a shadow into the future.

She threw the blanket aside and discovered a plaster cast on her leg. Damn! She pushed the bed rail down, swung her legs down, and stood, waiting for the dizziness to pass. She pulled the tubes and cables from her. The doctor was trying to talk her out of it, but she ignored him.

Tamara unwrapped her arms and hands, unrolling the bandages and casting them aside. Her hands and fingers were stiff, and the flesh around the many sets of stitches was red and puffy. They stung, but not enough to distract her from her growing sense of alarm. The doctor was saying something now about leaving against medical advice, or waiting until he brought discharge papers.

Could she remove her traces from the hospital's computers? Not without her *ai*. Which meant the man hunting her would find her, sooner rather than later.

She limped to the cabinet in the corner and found her clothes in a plastic bag labeled *biohazard*. She pulled the gown off and dropped it to her feet, and the doctor cleared his throat. She pulled her underwear and jeans on. The left leg had been cut away. Her white blouse was stiff with dried blood but she put it back on. She stuck her socks into her backpack, which was hanging next to the clothes, then dropped her boots to the floor. She stepped into one, but the other wouldn't fit over her cast so she grabbed it and her pack and limped out.

The hallway was quiet and deserted except for a nurse in pink scrubs who did a double take at the sight of Tamara. But she saw the doctor and moved on. Tamara paused, suddenly uncertain.

"Stop!" The doctor took her arm.

She tensed and was about to break his nose, but she forced herself to relax.

"Listen," he said, glaring at her. "You are this close to being declared a danger to yourself and others. Which gives me the power to put you in restraints. Is that what you want?"

Tamara returned the gaze of his blue eyes. She said, "I am leaving. You can either let me go, or try to stop me. If you try to stop me, well…" She tried to smile, but it came out as a grimace. "You are in a hospital, fortunately." She moved past him and limped to the elevator lobby.

"Wait," he said. "At least let me get you a wheelchair."

At the far end of the hall, the stairwell door opened and a dark figure stepped out, limned by the morning sunlight from the windows at the end of the hall.

Tamara caught her breath, threw her arms around the doctor, and buried her face in his chest. Over his shoulder she watched the figure slip into the room she had just vacated. The elevator pinged and opened, and she pulled the doctor inside and pressed the button for the first floor.

"Can you walk me out?" She gave him an innocent, endearing expression. "I'm scared." And she hugged him again. She wasn't good at this part, the emotional manipulation; that was her sister's specialty. Tamara preferred direct action.

The doctor returned the embrace awkwardly.

She breathed him in. Beneath the acrid tang of antiseptics, he had a good, clean smell to him. He was tall, and strong, and for a moment, she let herself enjoy the sense of safety in his arms, even though she knew it was false. He didn't realize she was protecting him, not the other way around. The id on his white coat said *Danny Nolan, MD PGY2*, a nice picture of him, and a barcode.

The elevator pinged and the doors slid open. Tamara tried to step out, but Danny held her back. She shoved him away with such force he staggered and half fell against the wall. She reached into her pack for her flechette gun.

It was gone. Shit!

She kicked his legs out from under him and he fell. She landed on his chest and dug her fingers under his jaw, finding the nerve clusters. He gasped.

"Listen," Tamara said. "I need to leave. Now. Someone is hunting me and I am in danger."

"I believe you," he whispered, gazing at her with his blue eyes.

The speed with which he agreed startled her. She stood and held out her hand, and helped him up. They stared at each other. She waited for him to do something stupid.

"You need to call the police," he said.

She'd anticipated that. "The man after me is a cop. He's my ex and he has a lot of friends."

He pursed his lips. He pressed the button and the elevator doors opened. Tamara followed him into the lobby, which was bright and busy.

She hobbled through the lobby and he followed. She tried to anticipate the assassin's path. He'd find her gone and then... check adjacent rooms? Someone would see him eventually. He could leave, and return in regular clothes to keep searching.

The double doors hummed as they slid open, and humid air heavy with exhaust fumes swept around them. Tamara scanned the area with tight, tense, hyper-vigilance. But no attack came.

The doctor stopped and she got the impression he was going no further.

"Please," she said, feeling far too vulnerable. "Can you take me to a motel?"

He hesitated. "I have duties."

"Please?" She made her voice plaintive, and tears appeared in her eyes. They were not honest tears, and for some reason she felt unscrupulous using them on him. But she needed help right now, and she trusted him.

Danny pursed his lips. He stared at her, baffled, with an expression that would have been endearing had she not been so distracted. He sighed. He took his phone from his pocket and dialed it. She tensed, but she felt he would not betray her now.

"Cai," he said. "I need you to cover for me. Yes, I know what time it is. Yes, it's important. Yes, it's a woman." His eyes met Tamara's and she unaccountably blushed and looked away. "Thanks Cai. I owe you."

Danny led her out to a red motorcycle sitting in the midst of luxury sedans. He removed his white coat and stethoscope, folded the coat around the instrument and handed it to her.

He mounted the motorcycle and kicked it into life, then held out his hand to help her up. She sighed in relief as they left the parking lot.

"Turn here," Tamara said. She had no destination in mind yet. Losing someone in time was a lot like losing someone in space. Turns, unexpected directions, and covering your tracks. Fortunately this was an older vehicle so it probably didn't have a GPS system. That reminded her: "Can I use your phone?"

He took it from the holster on his hip and handed it to her. She threw it off the bridge they were crossing.

"What the hell!" he shouted.

"Turn here," she said.

Instead, he pulled into a grocery store parking lot and rolled to a stop. "Get off."

Tamara buried her face against his shoulder and started sobbing.

He sighed and the bike began to move again. "You're crazy," he said. "I need to return you to the hospital and put you in a straitjacket."

"No! Please. I need your help." She tried to fill her voice with vulnerability, but she wasn't as good at the manipulation as Kyren was. She squeezed his shoulders. That's when she realized one of the stitches in her hand had torn, and blood smeared her palm. She stared at it, distracted.

He grunted. "You need help, that's for sure."

She wiped her hand on her torn jeans and clenched her fist to cut off the flow.

She directed him in a chaotic route for ten minutes and then had him enter a covered parking garage. The interior was dark and deserted. He pulled into a spot and turned the bike off.

Tamara climbed off the motorcycle and turned to him. "What happened to me?" she asked. He stared at her, so she clarified: "I came in with lacerations and a hole in my leg. Nothing life threatening. But now I'm... broken."

Danny surprised her by pulling his coat from her grasp. She tensed, but he just opened his stethoscope and put it on. "You should have told me. Are you having shortness of breath? Chest pains?" He stood. He reached out, unbuttoned the top of her blouse, and pressed the cold metal disk to her chest. If he heard her heart start to beat a little faster, he didn't say anything. "Are you feeling faint?"

"No." She pushed him away, feeling a little flushed.

"Well, your heart sounds good," he said. "No light headedness? Dizziness?"

"Danny," she said. "What happened to me?"

He removed the stethoscope from his ears. He gazed at her, then said, "I will tell you, but answer me first: what happened to you?"

Tamara thinned her lips in frustration. "I was mugged."

He regarded her with his sweet blue eyes. "By a plate glass window?"

"He shot me. I jumped through the window to get away."

"The wound on your leg was perfectly circular, through and through; no burns and no impact trauma."

"I don't know what he shot me with."

"And where did this happen?"

"Just down the street from the hospital. Now tell me what happened!" Tamara glared at the skepticism in his face.

"Miss Decaire," he said. "Twenty-four hours ago, you were dead."

It was her turn to gape at him. He couldn't be referring to her encounter at the library. "From what?"

"From the cardenolide in the leg wound."

Ah. Her shoulders sagged. The assassin had come a lot closer to killing her than she'd realized. That explained why her *ai* was dark. The shock of a defibrillator.

She had to hide. And she had to convince this man to hide with her. If he returned to his life and job now, the assassin would track her through him.

"Do you have cash?" she asked. He frowned and shook his head. Tamara dug into her backpack and pulled out a wad of money and handed it to him. "Okay. There's a motel across the street. Go get a room, but don't use a card and don't give your name."

Danny sighed. He gazed at her with pursed lips, then stamped out of the garage.

Tamara closed her eyes and wrapped her aching arms around herself to still her trembling. She was rattled, and she had to regain control. She'd been careless and now she was trapped and helpless until she recovered her *ai*.

Danny returned with a key and a room number. He handed the key and money to Tamara with the air of someone who was about to wash their hands of a problem. She reached out and placed her hand on his arm.

"Please come with me."

He studied her, the appeal in her eyes, her lips, her chest where she had not re-buttoned her blouse.

She leaned on him as they walked to the motel. The room was dim and cool and had a moldy lemon smell. He led her to the bed and eased her down. But when he tried to release her hand, she held on.

"Stay with me," she said. "Please?"

"Tamara…"

"Please. I'm afraid." She was, but not for the reason he believed. This room was safe for her only as long as he was here.

He sat on the bed and she lay back, holding his hand. She closed her eyes as weariness filled her like ice water. She knew it was the activity of the nanites, using her energy to heal her wounds. She was very hungry, but lethargy muted it.

"Promise you'll be here when I wake up. Don't leave."

"I promise," he said.

She didn't trust him that much. She should do something to make sure he didn't leave. Knock him out or something. As she considered it, her consciousness faded.

Catena 2

Tamara's iron grip on my hand slackened as she fell into a deep slumber. I held on for a while and thought about the mad turn of events. When I knew she was sound asleep, I checked her pulse and felt her forehead for a fever. Physically, she seemed fine, or at least as good as could be expected.

I gazed down at her. What in the world am I doing? I should leave. Go back to work. But no. This woman had a persuasive sincerity to her. I could tell she was withholding information, but I believed her when she said her life was in danger. And I believed her when she said she was frightened. And I more than half-believed she needed me to stay here with her. But why?

"Who are you?" I said out loud. I had an inexplicable impulse to protect her. From what? Whoever poisoned her. Whoever was trying to kill her. Her ex? I doubted that. That was too easy a fabrication for her. Who then? Most people did not have murderous enemies who would persist in hunting them down.

So what do I do? Wait with her like she wants? Call for help? Call who? Cai was covering for me? I didn't have many other friends. Not close friends.

The thought of waiting here idly while she slept repelled me. I had to do something. I hated idleness.

The first thing I did was pull the blanket over her, and take her single boot off. I checked to make sure she hadn't torn open any of her sutures. The one on her hand was broken, but the bleeding had stopped. When I satisfied myself that her condition would not deteriorate, I departed. I left my coat and stethoscope there next to her to reassure her that I'd be back.

I wasn't sure what I meant to do as I left the motel; I was just glad to be moving in some direction, any direction. I returned to my bike and rode out of the garage. I rode for a while without paying much attention to where I was going. Riding like this, with no destination and no agenda was my favorite way to clear my mind.

I spotted an old payphone outside a convenience store. I stopped. I couldn't remember Cai's number so I called the main number. "Doctor Cai Vaughn, please." He would be working my shift in the E.R., so he was probably going to be too busy to answer.

"Danny!" Cai said. "Did you really leave with a patient who went AMA? Okoro is livid."

I grimaced. "It's a crazy story, buddy." I gave him a summary of the situation. "So now she's hiding at a motel and thinks if I go back to work the guy will get to me."

"Wow," said Cai. "Then you're not going to believe this. Just a few minutes after you left, some guy showed up and asked for her by name. Said he was her brother."

"No shit?" A cold breath of disappointment escaped. Maybe she really was just a lunatic. "You get a name? A description?"

"No name. But pretty."

"Pretty?"

"Yeah, the secretary and nurses all said he was the prettiest man they'd ever seen. Tall, long blond hair. Model pretty. And an accent. They all agreed he wasn't American. Possibly a German or Scandinavian accent. Sorry, bro. That's all the info I have."

"Hmmm," I said. "This woman has an accent too, not strong, but definitely there. Her driver's license said New York, but she's not from there."

"International spies," Cai said melodramatically. "Oops. Gotta go, bud. Duty calls!"

"Right," I said with a snort after I hung up. Spies. Not likely. Should I go to the cops? Or the Feds? I suspected Tamara would not agree with either of those choices. And why in the world am I so concerned with her opinion?

Spies. I thought about the toy gun from her backpack. She'd reached for it in the elevator but it wasn't there. What had I done with it? It was on the table next to my recliner.

I felt the need to see it again. Maybe I'd missed something. I mounted my bike and rode home. There were no police cars around, and no suspicious people. No one who looked like a spy. Nothing tripped my absurd nascent paranoia. I parked close to the stairs and dashed up to my door. It was locked. Reality two—paranoia zero.

I walked in. Something, a change in air current, an unfamiliar smell, warned me a moment before a hard grip caught my neck and bent me over the coffee table. I saw my shocked expression reflected darkly in the glass table, and behind me, a figure leaned over me.

"Where is she?"

The voice had an odd, strong accent.

I'm not a weak man, but the way the assailant had me bent over, I couldn't get leverage to push back.

"Who?" I gasped. The grip tightened on my neck and I winced. "I don't know! I left her at some motel on Park." I lied about the street names. "Park and Miller."

The grip dug into my neck, pressing against nerves so hard I started to see flashes of light and felt as if I would go unconscious. I cried out, trying to kick backward.

Suddenly I was free, and staggered away from my attacker. I turned, my fist clenched. The man sported long, straight platinum blond hair that tumbled around his shoulders. He was about my height, and wore a buttoned brown trench coat. The word *pretty* fit perfectly. And he seemed extraordinarily young, barely out of his teens. But his black eyes seemed so cold and filled with dispassion that I had to force down a shiver.

"If you deceive," the man said in his strange, exotic accent. "You shall lament your existence."

"Right," I said, glaring at him. I was ready to beat the shit out of him.

The man gazed at me.

"The Country Club," I said. "That was the name of the motel. Room twelve."

The pretty man's eyes narrowed. Then he seemed to glance away. Abruptly his form lost some of its substance, like a musical chord losing its notes one at a time. It seemed to happen in slow motion, but in less than a second, the man was gone.

I gaped at the spot where he'd stood. "Oh damn. Oh, goddamn."

Catena 1

Tamara woke abruptly, and as she feared, Danny was gone. Damn! And her *ai* was still offline. She felt better physically, but that only gave her strength to act on her panic.

It was dark outside. She must have slept through the day.

How long had Danny been gone? How long would it be before the assassin caught up to him? It doesn't matter how long it took, however, because he could then *peregrinate* back to this very room on this very day. Which meant she had to leave. Now.

She thrust her good leg into her boot, grabbed the other boot and her backpack, and left the room. It was a humid night filled with cricket songs and car engines. She limped toward the closest swathe of darkness beyond the parking lot lights, wincing at the rocky gravel that jabbed her bare foot.

"Tamara!"

Danny was there, walking across the gravel. She half-limped half-ran to him and threw her arms around him. The delight of seeing him made her giddy.

But he said, "Let's go." His urgency startled her. He led her to his bike, mounted, helped her up without another word, kicked the motorcycle to life, and raced out of the parking lot. They sped down the streets, turning at random points, running stoplights like he was fleeing from the police. For nearly half an hour they rode through the city, ending up in a dark, seedy part of town and a disreputable motel. He strode into the office and emerged a minute later with a key, and they made their way to a hot, dingy, rancid-smelling room.

He made sure the grey curtains were shut completely and turned to her. She tried to read his intent in his face, but saw only doubt and apprehension.

"Tell me," he said. "Everything. No cover stories and no hedging."

She hesitated. She couldn't tell him the truth. He wouldn't believe it. But the way he stared at her. Something had rattled him. It could not have been the assassin. Could it? "Did he find you?"

His eyes narrowed. "He claimed he was your brother."

Tamara gaped at him. "Describe him!"

"Tall. Long blond hair. Arrogant. Strong." Almost as an afterthought he said, "Pretty."

Relief swept through her so abruptly she almost laughed. "Where!"

He frowned at her reaction. "My apartment. Are you saying—"

"My brother, yes," she said. Then she did laugh, a chuckle of relief and gratitude that Julian had come looking for her. She felt safer now just knowing he was here, in this time and place. If her *ai* worked, she could call him. But knowing she would see him soon comforted her and allowed her to relax. She stepped to Danny and hugged him, trying to instill in him her sense of deliverance. But he was unbending.

"Okay," she said. "I will tell you everything. But first…" She stepped away and started to unbutton her blouse, and was rewarded by the widening of his eyes. She suppressed a giggle. "I'm going to take a bath. I feel unkempt." She smiled at his baffled expression. "When I am done we can talk more." She grabbed her backpack and limped to the bathroom.

"Don't get the cast wet," he said from behind her. She wondered how closely he was watching her, and she flushed.

She closed the door and set the backpack in the sink. She showered first, not caring if she got the cast wet. After she felt clean, she turned the shower off and the hot water to full, and set the stopper.

Clouds of steam wafted around her as the tub filled. She wrapped her hair in a towel and spread another on the edge of the tub. She sat and lowered her cast-encased leg into the tub, hissing at the sting.

The cast was already starting to soften on the edges, and turned the water cloudy. She let it soak for half an hour, testing it occasionally, then used a penknife from her pack to cut the top edge of the cast and peel it away. It came off easily, revealing a red, puffy, stitched wound on each side of her leg. She rinsed her leg off, but when she tried to drain the tub the plaster in the water clogged the drain, leaving a motionless pool of grey-white water.

She toweled off and put on clean panties and a t-shirt. She threw her bloody clothes in the trash.

Danny saw her bare leg and glared at her.

"Forget about a shower," she said. "The tub is filled with plaster goop."

"Crazy woman," he muttered.

She came to him and took his hands. "Please don't leave me tonight. I don't want to be alone." She hugged him hard. He held her and patted her awkwardly. She knew he could feel her soft curves, and she pressed herself into him like a second skin, resting her head on his chest. His heart was beating faster. She inhaled his smell and indulged in the pure tactile experience of him. He took a deep breath of her as well, scents of soap and floral shampoo.

I'm yours, her body language said.

He put his hand on my head, brushed it across my wet hair. "I'll stay." He took her shoulders and pushed her to arms length. "Because you are going to answer my questions."

She stared at him and felt her face grow warm. "Are you ready to believe what I tell you, Danny Nolan?" She narrowed her eyes. "Young, confident, poised as you are will you be able to accept the truth?"

His cocked his brow in an infuriatingly composed way. "I watched your... brother disappear right before my eyes, hon, so my capacity to accept what you say might surprise you."

Tamara sighed. Yes, Julian didn't care about trying to hide their capabilities from the natives. Her defensiveness sagged and she sank to the bed. She wasn't ready for this. She was required to keep her Family's existence secret. But...

Catena 2

"I can't prove anything to you," she said. "Not yet. My *ai* isn't operational."

"Your eye?" I stepped closer to peer into her face, looking for damage.

"No, my *ai*. Artificial intelligence. An information processor. Here." She tapped the crown of her head. "The electrical discharge of the defibrillator disabled it."

"You have a computer in your head." I tried to keep the amazement out of my voice.

She nodded. "A microscopic one. You are familiar with nanotechnology?"

I knew a little, but—"I didn't know the technology had advanced so far."

"It hasn't."

I looked for the slight smile or glint in her eye that indicated she was being ironic. I didn't see it.

Her face was serious, "I would prefer to wait until I can prove what I say."

"You talk," I said. "Let me worry about proof."

My bull-headedness apparently annoyed her. "Fine," she snapped. "I am from a planet about one hundred light years from here, and from about a thousand years in the future." She glared into my eyes.

I absorbed that. Time-travel. Shit. Really? I wanted to give her a look of pure disdain, but I remember her brother disappearing right before my eyes. But... how was it possible? A part of me felt this was some great hoax. Or con. A con for what? I didn't have anything, or access to anything. Could the disappearing trick have fooled me? Sure. How? Beats the hell out of me. Okay. It was possible, though, so file it away in the back of my mind. But time-travel? How did one prove or disprove that?

"So you aren't from here, Earth, twenty-first century?"

"No."

"Who is the current president?"

She frowned. "I don't remember," she said, her voice heavy with reluctance. "With my *ai* offline, I can't access my *athenaeum*." She used a Greek word for 'library'.

"Then why are you here?"

Tamara regarded me. He could tell she was loath to open up to him, but he just held her gaze. He could wait the truth out of her. She would tell him because she trusted him. He could sense it in her expression and body language.

She said, "I belong to a… an organization that works to preserve the *natus* timeline."

"Natus?"

"The natural timeline. We keep others from changing the past in an effort to change the future."

"Well shit," I said. "I'm glad someone is!"

Her eyes narrowed, but she saw the twinkle in my eye and her tension eased. "You aren't reacting the way I'd expect you to."

I suppressed a wry smile. "I watched a man disappear right before my eyes. That demolishes a lot of skepticism."

"So you believe me?"

"No." She glared at me and I grinned. "You have me at my most open-minded right now, but I haven't reached a conclusion on how crazy you really are."

In spite of herself, Tamara laughed. "Very well, but this crazy woman is starving. Dinner?"

"There's a Chinese place around the corner. You wait here. I'll go."

"Use cash," she said.

I paused. "My name would be recorded in their system. And anyone patient enough to search for it…"

"Would find it eventually," she said. "And then be able to return to this area at this point in time. I call it casting a shadow into the future."

"So if we told your brother in the future where we were, he could show up right here and now." I looked around, suddenly expecting Julian to appear.

"He could," Tamara said with disinclination that surprised me. "But he can't. It's forbidden."

I frowned at her. Forbidden? I couldn't wrap my mind around that. "You will explain that when I get back?"

She nodded and I left the room. The humid night air slapped me in the face, as did the faint smell of rot from a trash dumpster at the edge of the parking lot. I wanted to believe her. I sure as hell did! How incredible would it be to come face-to-face with the future? What was life like a thousand years from now? Besides clearly advanced technology. I was so energized by the prospect that I realized I was walking faster that I normally do.

A dog started barking off to my right and I stopped, peering in that direction and I held my breath. Nothing but insects clouding around streetlights. A car pulling out of the nearby subdivision. A couple in the distance walking slowly holding hands. I shook my head and resumed my mission. I ordered the food and waited for it. I noticed a security camera in the lobby of the restaurant and turned away from it. A shadow into the future, she'd called it. I wondered if the camera had caught my face. And would a time-traveler-hunter review the video in a day or a week or a year and then jump back to here and now? I looked around, but the place was quiet. A family with kids dined at one of the tables, the mother shushing the exuberant children. A man sat at another table reading a folded newspaper, his dinner half eaten. A trio of youths sauntered by on the sidewalk in front of the restaurant. A car horn sounded. It took a case of the paranoias for me to notice these details I usually took for granted.

The dinner arrived in a plastic bag and I left. I entered the next-door convenience store and bought a six-pack of beer, then returned to the motel room.

Tamara was still there, sitting on the edge of the bed. A part of me had expected the room to be empty. That she was still there gladdened me.

Catena 1

After Danny left for the restaurant, Tamara drew a deep breath. She should not be doing this. Giving him answers. The Family insisted on secrecy. But she needed his cooperation, at least until her *ai* returned, or until Julian found her. Fortunately, she trusted him. What's more, she liked him.

He seemed to take longer than she anticipated, and anxiety knotted in her gut. Footsteps sounded outside the door and adrenaline rushed through her. The key clicked and the door opened to reveal Danny, and her concerns flowed out of her with a relieved sigh.

They shared plastic containers of sweet-and-sour chicken and orange beef. Tamara ate ravenously, and when he finished, she ate what he left.

He asked, "Do you eat like that all the time?"

"Only when I've been shot."

Danny's eyes swept her figure. "You must have quite the metabolism."

His attention suddenly made her self-conscious. "I do. More than you realize."

He pondered that. "Nanotechnology?"

She nodded, pleased at how quickly his mind worked.

He'd also brought a six-pack of beer. She drained one and half of a second before he said:

"Easy!"

She slowed, although it would take more than a couple of beers to affect her.

"Feeling better?" he asked.

"I am." She smiled at him.

He pulled her gun from his back pocket. She kept her face expressionless. "It looks like a toy, but given what you told me, I expect you to show me it is not."

She glared at him, despite her relief that she had not lost her weapon. "How long have you been planning this?"

He grinned at her. "You wanted a way to show me proof." He tossed it to her.

"It's a flechette gun," she said. "It shoots darts about three centimeters long and harder than steel."

"The wound in your leg?"

Tamara nodded. "Whoever shot me had a gun like this."

He looked skeptical. "It doesn't work."

"It's keyed to my bioelectric signature."

He watched her.

She pointed it toward the bathroom and pulled the trigger. The gun jerked with three quick snaps so close together that they seemed like a single sound. Three holes less than two centimeters apart appeared in the wall, and the bathtub rang from a heavy blow.

Danny jumped. "Shit!"

Tamara limped to the bathroom. The three holes in the side of the tub were spaced farther apart than those in the wall. She thrust her hand into the grey-white water and plaster goop and found one of the darts. She pulled it out and handed it to Danny, who had followed her.

He took the dripping black dart from her and wiped the goop off. It was pristine and undeformed, a tiny nail with miniscule fins. It wasn't even scuffed. He frowned at her, at the holes in the tub and the wall, and again at the dart.

She took the flechette from him and held it and the small gun together for comparison. "How many shots do you think this holds?"

He pondered it. "Six, maybe?"

"Each time I pull the trigger it shoots three." She tossed the dart to him then pointed the gun at the ground between her feet. She pulled the trigger and with a snap a hole appeared in the tile and the concrete below it. She pulled the trigger again and the hole widened, puffing dust and debris into the air. She shot repeatedly, and each time the hole widened a little more. She pulled the trigger ten times, then shifted the aim and continued to shoot. She shot ten more times, then shifted the aim again and made another hole. This time she just kept shooting as she raised her gaze to watch him.

He stared in amazement as she continued to shoot and dust rose around them. She kept shooting flechettes into the foundation of the building and watched him until he held up his hand.

"Stop. Where… is the ammo coming from?"

"An *aleph* field generator."

"A…?"

"A Raslan field. Also called a dynamic field. An *aleph* field is the interstices of three other fields that form the sub-atomic structure of matter."

"Wait." Now he frowned. "I know enough physics to…" He pressed his lips together.

"Amil Raslan, the scientist who first theorized the existence of *aleph* fields, won't be born for another twenty years."

"Right," Danny said. "Time travel. Okay. So time is a field?"

"Actually, time as you perceive it is the interaction of nine dynamic fields, three sets of three. Dynamic fields almost always interact in sets of three. There seems to be a natural stability to the configuration. Dynamic fields are the fundamental building blocks of nature. The interactions of the fields generate quantized Raslan tensors which carry the fundamental forces of spacetime. *Aleph* fields are comprised of three other fields: *yodh* and *nun* fields carry the nuclear and electromagnetic forces, and *kaph* fields impart mass."

"Like the Higgs field?" Danny said quickly, eager to prove that he was not as ignorant as he felt.

Tamara gave a non-committal shrug. "Higgs theory only touches the surface. It will take another hundred years for humans to see the full picture. But this century is one of discovery and innovation. It's one of the reasons I like living here."

Danny scratched his chin. "I was going to ask why you are here. You live here?"

Tamara nodded. "Each member of my family lives in a different time and place. We are spread out. That way any unexpected change in the timeline doesn't affect all of us."

"Yes!" Danny said, snapping his fingers. "That's been bothering me too. The paradoxes. How do you get around them?"

"There are no paradoxes." Tamara could not help but grin at his skeptical look. "*Peregrination* removes us from the *natus* timeline."

"Para-?"

"It means to travel from one set of spacetime coordinates to another."

"So… if you kill your own grandfather…"

Tamara giggled, causing Danny to glare at her. "They my grandfather is dead and I am still there, standing over his body."

"And you never existed."

"In the *natus* timeline, that is true. But when I *peregrinate*, I establish a new *catena* in the timeline where I arrive."

"*Catena.* I know that word. Latin for *chain.*"

Tamara nodded. "My Family tends to see existence, and everything in it, as a series of chain links, bundled and entwined together like the individual fibers of a rope. Together these *catenae* comprise the whole of reality, extending from the beginning of the universe to its end."

"Hmmm," Danny said. "I've heard that analogy before to illustrate Determinism."

"Yes. We mean it in the same way. *Catenae* are the sum total of cause and effect moments."

"So you are immune to cause and effect?"

"No, I am saying cause and effect do not follow me when I *peregrinate*. Changes to *catenae* only propagate forward through the *tau* field. The rule of thumb is this: any change I make to the timeline does not change me."

Danny considered that. "It does not change you, because your… *catena* doesn't follow you when you travel through time?"

Her wry expression told him his grasp of the concept was still imperfect.

"Okay," he said. "Changes you make do not change you. That's easy enough. But a change someone else makes would?"

"Possibly," Tamara answered. "If you *peregrinated* to the moment when I was attacked and prevented it from happening, then from my perspective this conversation never happens. I proceed with my life in Manhattan. From your perspective, however, the events are real; you don't forget this conversation, or me. You have changed my *catena*. But by changing my timeline, you have also changed your own. I never come to your hospital. So you never meet me. So you go on with your life. This is why we are very careful about making changes, and work to keep others from making changes."

Danny frowned. "I'm not following."

"You are Danny Nolan," she said. "An extraordinary and unique man. But if you change your *catena*, and are unchanged by that change; what is the result?"

He considered that. "I am there. But I am also here. I am… two?"

43

"Yes. Changing your own timeline results in two Dannys. The Changer and the One Changed. We call the One Changed an *analogue*, which is a dry way of saying you have created an identical copy of yourself. We have strict rules that keep us from doing anything that would create an *analogue* of ourselves."

"Because an *analogue* Tamara would…" Danny struggled with the idea.

"She would be me," Tamara said. "In every way she would be a copy. A perfect copy. And who could tell her she isn't me? From her perspective, she would be me, and would begrudge any assertion that she was not Tamara."

"And this is the reason we can't tell your brother in the future to come get us now?"

"Because we would be both there in the future and here now. It would create *analogues* of us."

Danny scratched his chin, thinking about that. "It is strange, hearing the words 'there', 'here', and 'now' in a conversation about time travel."

That reminded Tamara that she should not be telling him anything. Or at least, telling him the bare minimum.

"What's wrong?" he asked.

She didn't mean for it to show on her face, either. She finished her beer. "I'm tired. And stuffed." She put the trash away and then climbed into the bed, which squeaked under the motion. She lay back, closed her eyes, and patted the spot beside her.

He didn't move except to take another beer and open it. The cap rattled on the table next to the bed. She peered at him through half-open eyed. He sat in the chair, drinking his beer and watching her. She felt unexpectedly comfortable under his gaze. If he'd wanted to take advantage of her, he'd have done it already. She smiled inwardly He'd asked for nothing in return. And what he did want… well… she'd seen the way he looked at her, and she liked it.

Also to her surprise, she really did start to fall asleep. The nanites registered her inactivity and digestion, and geared up to accelerate the repairs to her body. A good night's sleep and she'd be back to normal.

She dreamed she was in her old skiff orbiting a rotating black hole she had nicknamed "the Pond" because of the blue-shifted light from its outer photon sphere. Only this time her *nun-tau* drive had failed and she was falling toward the event horizon. Her brother Julian was trying to reach her, but his ship slowed more and more as it approached, and she knew he wouldn't reach her in time.

Catena 2

I finished all the beers as I watched Tamara sleep. She seemed particularly vulnerable now, her eyes closed, wearing nothing but a t-shirt and panties. She wanted me to join her in the bed. And I sure as hell wanted to. I wanted to go over and wake her with a kiss I know she would have returned with enthusiasm. I'd never met such a vibrant woman. Even wounded and off-balanced as she was, she radiated energy like a sun. Instead I just watched over her and weighed the pros and cons of being a gentleman.

But after an hour or so I knew I needed more beer. Actually I needed gin, but I didn't see a liquor store around. I quietly left the room and walked to the convenience story. It was getting close to midnight. The world had grown quieter, though that dog was still barking from the nearby neighborhood. A siren wailed in the distance, which reminded me that I ought to be on duty right now. Why was I doing this, again?

Well, if she was telling the truth...

I returned to the image of her brother disappearing right before my eyes. How could that be faked? He had been there. His smell, his iron grip on my neck, his unrecognizable accent. Well, if they were from a thousand years in the future, then of course I would not recognize the accent. It made self-consistent sense. It was just an impossible premise. But if it *was* possible, then I sure as hell wanted to know more! And that gun. I could still smell the concrete dust the flechettes had kicked up as they burst into the foundation of the motel.

That had been very real. I bought another six-pack and started back to the motel. I reached the edge of the gravel parking lot and looked toward our room.

The door was open.

As I stared, a burst of bright blue light filled the room and then was gone, like someone had used a camera. Cold nausea filled my gut, and I knew even as I started to run. I charged into the room. Her backpack and boots were still there. Her gun was not.

I sat on the bed for an eternity. I don't know when, but I started drinking the beers, which I'd somehow managed to hang on to. I poured the beers into the crushed darkness of my spirit and they disappeared as if into a black hole. No help at all.

She was gone. The most amazing woman I'd ever met. She left me. No. Her boots were still here. Someone took her. She would not have willingly left without seeing me. Would she? I don't know. And she left her backpack.

I sprang up and grabbed the backpack. I unzipped it and poured the contents on the bed. Clothes. A tool kit. A pen knife. Ah! A Cell phone. An old flip phone. I opened it. It only had three numbers in memory. I dialed the first. It went straight to voice mail without an introduction. I dialed the second and a got an answering message telling me that Tony and Tina's Pizzaria was closed for the evening. The third number rang continuously and was never answered. Shit. I pocked the phone and looked for anything else that might give me a clue. I found it.

Her driver's license with her home address. I gave the contents of the pack a final cursory inspection, grabbed the wad of cash, and was about to race out of the room.

Suddenly, with a faint blue flash so quick I might have imagined it, two people stood in the room with me.

I stopped, nonplussed.

The girl had long, straight golden hair and wore a silver-grey jumpsuit. She seemed no older than twenty.

"Danny Nolan," she said with the same exotic accent as Tamara and her brother.

The man with her was taller but he could have otherwise been her twin except his hair was short and spiky. He wore black pants and a tunic of rich purple. He carried a flechette gun and his eyes flicked continuously around the room at through the open door. He had a dangerous, coiled-serpent feel to him.

"Are you hurt?" the girl asked. She walked around the bed. She radiated genuine concern as her gaze raked his figure. She reached up to press cool fingers to my forehead, but I shook her off.

"Who are you?"

The man said something in a language I didn't understand, and the girl said, "He appears uninjured."

The man said something else and I heard him say "Tamara."

"Where is she!" I demanded, clenching my fists.

"Fear not, Danny," said the woman. "We will find Tamara." She touched my arm.

My world flipped upside down and inside out. Vertigo and a falling sensation swept over me, and I clutched at the girl in a panic. Then I stood on solid ground again. I would have fallen from the dizziness had she and man not steadied me. Holy shit. Holy fucking shit! The sensation stunned me as much as the vista that greeted me. Holy hell! I gaped as nausea churned in my stomach. My legs trembled.

We stood in a green, sunlit valley under a cloudless blue sky. Ahead of us in the distance rose the silhouette of a mountain, bluish gray from atmospheric haze. The glittering skyscrapers of a city rose from the slope. Aircraft glided and flitted over the city like tiny insects. At the summit of the mountain an immense light-filled tower soared into the sky, rising a mind-numbing height above me, appearing to reach all the way into space. I stared up at it and vertigo again threatened to send me reeling. The sight was both impossible and stunningly real.

Farther in the distance, atop other mountain peaks, rose other towers, a series of space elevators marching to the horizon and beyond like the spokes of a wheel. From each of the towers flashes of light erupted and flickered, and bright blue-white beams of coherent light momentarily leap between adjacent towers.

It's real. It's true. It's all true.

We stood at the head of the valley at least forty kilometers from the city. A warm breeze blew through the vale, heavy with an exotic flowery scent. Groves of trees around them were heavy with white blossoms.

It's real.

"The city is Siola," the girl said. "Capital of the Alosian Republic. This planet is called Vaerdine, or, on navigator charts, Alosia Three Alpha."

"This…" I began, staring at the line of towers. But I didn't know what to say. I shook his head.

"Come," said the man.

Just to the right of us lay a circular platform of blue metal embedded in the ground. The man stepped onto it and the girl led me to it. It was just a disk of metal, three meters in diameter, with no apparent control system. I wasn't sure if it would sink into the ground like an elevator, or rise into the air like a flying carpet. Instead, my world turned upside down again, and I again had the panicked falling sensation.

Good God!

Some kind of natural cavern burst into existence around us. Bright light emanated from a yellow globe that gave the appearance of a miniature sun hovering near the top of the cave. The light limned the rough, natural stone that formed the ceiling and walls. We stood on the same blue metal platform or one identical to it, in the center of the cavern.

To my left along the wall stood an array of black consoles in front of which sat a pair of chairs. Three openings in the cavern revealed corridors to other parts of the complex. A brightly lit room overlooked the central chamber through broad windows.

The blond twins glanced at each other. The man dashed into one of the corridors, calling out "Yana!" There was no response.

The girl took my arm and led me to one of the chairs, and sat in the other facing me. Bars of lights on the black consoles began to glow with barely perceptible purple and orange lights.

"What's wrong?" I asked. She appeared worried. She held out her left hand to the consoles, and reached out to place her right hand on my forehead. A fully realized, true-color, three-dimensional image of my head appeared in the space before her left hand, startling me. I stared at it, and when I blinked, my image blinked. "Uh…"

"Be still," she said. She took both her hands and touched her fingertips to the image and began to manipulate it, rotating it, enlarging it, and then delving into it, stripping off the outer layers to look inside. I stared at it, at the blood vessels throbbing at my temple, then at the wrinkled grey matter of my brain in a spider web of capillaries. She zoomed in through the temporal lobes to a view of the amygdalae. They began to glow with a palette of blue colors.

"What is your name?" she asked in her light, accented voice.

"Danny Nolan," he said.

"Lie to me," she said, winking at him.

"My name is Forrest Gump."

The blue glow changed to a magenta color, then gradually returned to its original shade.

"How do you know Tamara?"

I told her the story, trying to leave nothing out. An orange glow appeared along some regions of the temporal lobes, but the blue remained constant. When I described her demonstration with the flechette gun, other regions took on a red glow. While I spoke, the girl reached up with her right hand to lay two fingers under the angle of my jaw where my carotid artery pulsed.

A sharp sting bit where she touched me, and I jumped. "Ow!" I raised my hand to my neck, checking it for blood, but there was nothing. She lowered her hands and the image disappeared. "What was that?"

"I injected you with nanites."

I glared at her. "I don't recall asking you to!" Nanites? She'd injected me with microscopic robots. The idea both intrigued and frightened me. Was that the brick red glow that flushed through my amygdalae, my fear?

"Alea!" The other man charged into the chamber, said something to the girl, then hurried down another corridor.

The girl jumped up as the image of my brain disappeared, and charged into the third tunnel. The two of them returned a minute later. They exchanged troubled expressions. The man frowned and shook his head. I had the sense they were communicating somehow.

A deep bell sound reverberated throughout the complex, and then another man stood in the chamber on the platform.

I shot to his feet. It was the long-haired asshole who'd assaulted me. I looked around for something to use as a weapon, but there was nothing. I clenched my fists and stamped toward the tall, pretty man. The newcomer regarded me with pure indifference.

"Where is she?" I demanded. "What did you do to her?"

The man crossed his arms and watched me bear down on him. His stance, his superior attitude, and the fact that he made no effort to retreat made me hesitate. What did he know that I did not?

I said to the girl, "This was the one chasing Tamara."

"Did you find her?" the girl asked in her accented English.

The newcomer answered her in a language that sounded like it should have been familiar.

I glanced from one to another, at their blond hair and angular faces.

"Who the hell are you people?"

They started talking to each other in their odd, almost familiar language, gesturing to the corridors. Then the other man who had been with the girl stepped onto the blue metal platform, and the two of them disappeared, leaving her alone with me.

"Come," she said to me. "There is food and a place to rest." She gestured to one of the corridors.

I didn't move. "Not until you tell me what's going on."

She came to me and took my hand, and led me out of the central cavern. "I will explain while you eat."

I wasn't hungry, but the promise of answers motivated me. She led me to a kitchen area. A light panel in the ceiling came on as we entered, and one of the boxes that might have been an oven started to blink a red light. She sat me down at a small round table with four chairs.

She smiled at me to put me at ease. "I am Alea. Those are my brothers, Paul and Julian. Julian was… unkind to you when you first met him."

"Yeah." I rubbed my neck, which still ached from his iron grip.

"Forgive him. He is the youngest of us, barely a hundred."

"Barely a hundred," I repeated, letting that sink in. "How old are you?"

"Paul and I are one hundred and seventeen."

"You don't look a day over twenty," I said. She laughed, even though I'd been serious. "Are you… immortal?"

"No. On Vaerdine, the life span is around two hundred and fifty. But for our Family it is at least twice that."

The way she said *our family* suggested she meant something more than a nuclear family. "Tell me about your family."

The oven chimed and she stood. She returned with a ceramic bowl and spoon. The bowl contained a soup pungent with odors I'd never encountered, mingled with smells that I did recognize and that made his mouth water. I stirred the steaming mixture, a brownish liquid with red and blue shapes that I assumed were vegetables. I tasted it. My jaw clenched at the exotic flavors, but I swallowed it, and the warmth that spread from my stomach felt good. I took another bite and concentrated on the strange flavors. This time my palate accepted it without protest. It wasn't bad. And it turned out I really was hungry.

"Our Family," Alea said, pondering that topic. "We… guard… time."

Tamara had said about the same thing. Here was my chance to detect any breaks in the internal consistency of this mad adventure.

I asked, "Guard it from what?"

"Whoever would change it. My Family--the older generation of my Family--participated in a misguided effort to change the *natus* timeline and ended up ruining two civilizations. The survivors repaired the timeline as best they could, and resolved to keep it from happening again." She gazed absently at her hands. "We spend our lives watching for, and undoing, anyone else's efforts to change time. When things go right, from the perspective of the would-be time-traveler, the technology just fails to work."

"And when things go wrong?"

"We have made enemies," she said quietly.

"How many are there of… your family?"

"Twelve. Six of the elder generation, six of the younger."

"And Tamara?"

"She is the second oldest of my generation."

"And one of your enemies is trying to kill her?"

A shadow crossed Alea's face. "Each of us has faced an attempt on our lives in the past two days. Even more unusual, we were each on different planets at different times in the *natus* timeline."

Thinking about this made my head throb. Or maybe it was the beer. "Any casualties?"

Alea gave a grim smile. "It is not easy to kill one of us."

I thought about Tamara, bloody and poisoned, in my ER and how close she had come to dying.

The deep bell sound echoed through the complex again. Alea stood. "Someone has returned."

"Alea!" a man shouted from down the corridor.

Alea ran from the kitchen. I followed.

Julian was carrying his brother Paul, who was bleeding from a dozen different wounds.

I immediately found myself in triage mode. Paul was suffering from numerous lacerations, but three closely space holes in his torso drew my focus as well as Alea's. She led us to another wing filled with medical devices, some I recognized, some I didn't.

Julian laid Paul out on the white, padded table and instantly a three-dimensional image overlaid Paul's body like a second skin. It glowed bright red at the site of the flechette wounds, and a fainter red over the other lacerations. An orange glow permeated the entire image. Numbers were projected into the space over the body, as well as other readouts. I frowned at them, trying to grasp their significance. Many of them seemed almost familiar. The heart sinus rhythm was obvious though. It was fast, but slowing.

Alea took some device that looked like a merger of a test tube and a gun, and injected something into the flechette wounds. The vividness of the red indicator overlaying the wound lessened.

I kept my attention on the heart rhythm, looking for the telltale signs. There! The T-wave was flattening. And a U-wave had appeared. I said, "There may be a cardenolide in the flechette wounds." Alea turned to me, startled. "It almost killed Tamara."

Alea stepped to a cabinet and pulled out a small, oval vial. I expected her to take a syringe as well. But she only gripped the vial in her right hand and pressed her index and middle fingers to the flechette wounds. I watched with a baffled frown. The image over the wound grew adulterated with a spreading grey haze that spread out from the wound, and the orange color of the image began to fade. She opened her hand. The vial was gone.

"The drug has been neutralized," Alea said. "Thank you, Danny." She proceeded to treat Paul's other wounds, cleaning them and then using a small rod that exuded an adhesive to close them. I watched, fascinated and pleased, my curiosity nearly overflowing.

"What happened?" She asked Julian, who watched her work from near the entrance, his expression emotionless. Julian answered in his strange, almost familiar language.

Alea turned to stare at him in surprise.

"What did he say?" I asked.

Alea answered, "Lerys was not there, but an assassin was. And he had a failsafe." She looked unnaturally pale now.

I frowned. "A what?"

"A transient field generator," she said. "If it detects a cessation of life signs, it will trigger a six-second jump back in time, giving the target a chance to react before a mortal wound is sustained."

"I take it these failsafes are not common?"

"No one has them," Alea said, shaken. "Only our Family." She said to Julian, "We need to warn the others." He nodded. She said, "Will you go to Beran?"

"No." Julian said.

"Julian."

He turned away and started down the corridor, saying something over his shoulder I thought I could almost comprehend.

Alea sighed and bent her attention to Paul. She touched her hand to his forehead. "His *ai* is dark. He must have been hit with an energy surge. But he's stable." She raised the rails on the bed. "I don't like the idea of leaving him, but we need to warn the others."

"We?" I said.

"I don't want to leave you alone either."

I wondered what I would do, on my own a thousand years beyond my time. The idea tingled within me. This is actually happening? I followed her to the chamber with the platform. She stepped onto it. I followed more carefully, holding my breath, my muscles tense.

The world flipped with the same unsettling falling sensation, and then we were again in the valley below the mountain city of Siola. Then Alea reached out and took my hand and the world tumbled again, going dark.

"Jeez!" I gasped, staggering as my equilibrium sloshed around inside me. Alea's hand steadied me. The world remained dark, but now a blue glow filled it. I looked up at an impossible night sky and gaped.

A glowing blue cloud filled the entire sky, not an atmospheric cloud, but a stellar one, and through it glittered thousands of stars, including three brilliant blue stars so bright they bathed the landscape in ghostly light. The landscape itself was starkly barren, covered with swathes of sand and bare rock outcroppings. A dry, cold wind blew from... Disorientation threatened to overwhelm me. An artificial geodesic dome ten meters high crouched on the lifeless land behind us. A warm golden light flowed from the doorway.

"Where—where are we?" I asked, looking up again at the dazzling blue stars.

"Alnilam Four," Alea answered. "Homeworld of the Shen, who call it Shenzhou."

She led me to the dome entrance, which opened into a short hallway which itself opened into a central workroom with a glass ceiling open to the amazing night sky. The workroom was messy and unkempt, tables with scattered papers and cups and dishes piled randomly."Doctor Beran!" Alea called out. She scanned the area uncertainly. "Wait here," she said and moved into another room. When she returned, her face was alarmed. "He is gone." She bit her lip.

"What's going on?" I asked. Her expression triggered an answering apprehension in me.

"I do not know," she said. "If he were here, in this time, and place, and conscious, he would hear my call with his *ai*. But he does not answer." She moved from room to room, shaking her head. She looked so rattled he wanted to go and comfort her.

"Beran," she said. "He's our founder. Our leader. And he is gone."

Catena 1

Tamara returned to consciousness, a dark, hollow consciousness bereft of her *ai*.

She was naked and lying on a block of ice; at least, it felt as cold as ice. She was spread-eagled, her wrists and ankles bound. A blindfold covered her eyes.

Soft steps to her right.

"I have awaited your return from the empty land of the unconscious." The voice was inhuman, machine generated.

She flinched at the light touch that trailed over her breast, paused to circle her nipple, and then slid down my abdomen. "Okay, pervert," she said. "Release me and I'll show you a good time."

Soft laughter, made creepier by the machine medium. "Bravado becomes you, my treasure."

She didn't recognize the voice through the artificial medium, but something about the speaker's cadence and choice of words triggered a sense of vague recognition, an almost-familiarity that made her shudder involuntarily.

"Feel free to struggle, Tamara. But your bonds are quite secure. And the electric current flowing through the table and through you is sufficient to neutralize your *ai*."

Ice shocked through her veins. He knew about her *ai*, and how to disable it. Impossible! The Family had guarded none of its secrets more carefully. Never could their enemies be allowed to learn that simple electric currents and discharges were their greatest vulnerabilities.

Which meant this bastard would have to die; more, he would have to be erased. She would have to learn enough about him to find out when and where to go to efface his *catena*.

"Who are you?" her voice seemed alarmingly rough with her anxiety. She forced herself to relax. Take it easy. Cooperate. Take what he gives. Endure. Eventually he would lower his guard enough. Tamara knew how to wait.

"Who are you?" the mechanical voice repeated. "Do you think you have given your life well?"

Tamara's throat tightened. If he killed her now, with her *ai* dark, all she would have is the failsafe, which would do nothing but send her back in time six seconds to experience it over and over. The transient field generator lacked the capability to do more than that. Usually it was enough to help a member of the Family avoid a mortal wound. But if Tamara were already helpless, she would remain helpless. And if the killer was not aware of the failsafe, he would strike the killing blow over and over, never realizing that he, like her, was trapped in an unending loop. It was small consolation for her to know she was trapping her killer with her, holding him in the loop until another member of her Family detected it and changed the *catenae* that converged together to manifest it. On the other hand, it might be the best way to trap him until the Family could deal with him.

"I know what you are thinking," said the cold voice. "But you have erred. When I *peregrinate* away, the loop will be localized to you, and you will die over and over and over, screaming. I will regret not being able to hear your death keen. I would relish it."

Speechless dread choked her. The realization that her captor knew about her failsafe, and how to use it to torture her, and the prospect of dying over and over with no surcease shook her to her core. How could their enemies know so much about them? And if they knew so much, then Tamara suspected she was not the only target. The entire Family was in jeopardy.

The alien voice laughed, as if he discerned her thoughts and mocked her for them. Then he left her to await her death.

But death did not come. Nothing came. She lay there, motionless, and was greeted only by silence and her own breaths. Her limbs began to ache from immobility. The aches became pain she tried to relieve by shifting, but eventually even that was not enough. The pain came, and grew, and did not leave. She called out, called for help, but her voice returned muffled. Wherever she was, no one would hear her. When the silence became difficult to endure, she began to talk to herself, then to sing, to tell herself stories and reminisce. She thought about Danny Nolan and that helped for a while. She liked him. She was attracted to him. He was smart, strong, and above all a good person. She imagined his blue eyes, intense and bright; his smile that tended toward wryness; his strong arms and hard shoulders. What had happened to him? Alarm caught in her throat. Had her captor killed him, or captured him? She hoped he was all right. She regretted that he had not taken the opportunity to have sex with her. She'd wanted him to. It would have been amazing. But even distracting herself with those erotic thoughts didn't last, and she returned again to herself, caught, bound, and alone.

Time passed. Hours. Days? She lost her sense of the passage of time. Where had her kidnapper gone? What if he never came back? The sense of isolation grew, and a looming sense of loneliness and helplessness. She screamed. She struggled against the bonds futilely. Pinned and alone. Finally, in her abject loneliness, she hoped for him to return. His mockery, his threats, any torture would be preferable to her sense of interminable isolation.

Hunger set in. And thirst. He was going to leave her to die like this, of thirst or starvation, a slow, slow death. Then her failsafe would kick in to allow her to relive the final six seconds of her misery over and over. She screamed until she could scream no more. She wept until she could weep no more. Resignation smothered her again and again, until her energy returned to struggle more. But finally resignation came and would not leave, and her mind lost itself in insensate, nascent psychosis and bouts of unconsciousness.

"Is it worth it?"

"What?"

"The Family never gave you a choice. You were chosen from birth to be their agent, to fight for their cause, to ameliorate their guilt. No one ever asked you about your dreams or ambitions or desires."

Tamara had never questioned her service to the Family. It was right. And necessary. Her loyalty was a fusion of love for her parents, respect for the Elders, and the sense of duty instilled in her by them.

"Is it worth it?"

"It is necessary!"

"Is it, my treasure?"

Tamara was not sure if the conversation was going on in her imagination or in reality. She had lost touch with reality.

"It is not necessary," said the mechanical voice of her captor. "You were wasted by the Family. Your talents, your energy, all wasted in a useless effort to defend Time. Well Time does not need defending, and Time communicates no appreciation for your labors. Herol Beren misled you. He misled the entire Family. The obsession to maintain one of an infinity of possible timelines is *his* madness. The rest of the Elders merely joined him out of gratitude. And then gave their children to him to shape into caricatures of himself, mindless beasts of burden carrying his personal demons."

Tamara had regained a bit of herself, enough to know her captor had rejoined her, and was trying to persuade her. And he knew enough about the Family that he could not be an enemy. He had to be a member of the Family. No! It could not be possible. She knew each and every one of her Family intimately, and the idea that one of them was a traitor felt impossible... an alien concept. How was it possible?

"Who are you?" she wasn't sure she spoke out loud.

A mechanical chuckle. "We have not reached that point in our conversation, my dear Tamara."

Again the voice seemed familiar. But who? It had to be Lor, Beran's son and the oldest of the children, an aloof, arrogant, and judgmental man. But how could it be Lor? He supported his father's mission more fiercely than anyone else. Or was it Paul, the most aggressive of the younger generation, and the one most vocal in criticizing Beran's policies? But he was loyal to his father Lerys, and Lerys supported Beran.

"There is something I want to do, first," said my captor. "I want to hurt you."

The mild way he said it made Tamara shiver. Then, as if her entire body remembered it was cold and hurting, she began to tremble uncontrollably.

"Good," the disembodied voice said, and she could hear the smile. "Good."

Tamara cried out in rage, and strained and jerked at the straps with mad frenzy, uncaring what damage she did to her limbs. After a time she stopped, exhausted, gasping for breath as her muscles spasmed and burned from the exertions.

"Is that all?" the vile voice said with amusement.

She whispered. "What do you want?"

"Ah," he said. "I have already made that clear, sweet Tamara. I must break you."

The platform she lay on began to vibrate, and produced a faint hum that buzzed in her eardrums and skull. The vibrations grew in intensity, but not in volume, and her flesh quivered as if thousands of ants were crawling over her. Then those ants began to bite. Itching, and then stringing, and then burning. Red hot needles began to stab into her flesh, scorching it, blistering it, injecting venom to make her muscles seize and her nerves shriek. Pain enveloped her like a blanket, a funeral shroud of acid, and then the pain became anguish.

She wasn't sure when she started screaming. She tried to lose herself in unconsciousness, but she couldn't. Her shattered spirit tried to shrink away from the torment but had nowhere to go, and degenerated into a mindless, quavering mass of suffering. Her soul gibbered, wept, and whined, and through it all, she imagined the avid gaze of her torturer.

Eventually her conscious mind fell passive and all that remained was the snarling wild animal of instinct, biting uselessly at parts of her body that hurt the most. In the end even that gave way to a wailing child longing for her mother's arms. Mama! She remembered her mother holding her and soothing her, and she buried her face in her mother's breasts and wept.

She don't know how long the pain went on. It could have been hour or days. The electronic pain stopped from time to time, and her captor would climb atop her and rape her. She started to enjoy these interludes, because they provided surcease. She even begged him to stay within her, as she relished the pleasure of the absence of pain. A small part of her watched the vile tableau in horror.

She died. She drowned in misery and dismay and her torturer returned her to life. He would hurt her and fuck her and hurt her more. And continually he would whisper sweet nothings to her, telling her how beautiful she was, how he loved her, how he would take care of her. He also led her in questioning her loyalty to the Family, and her dedication to her duty. He was breaking her, and she could not resist much longer. She clung to a piece of herself, walled off from the torture and the surcease and the madness, and defended it with all the strength she could muster.

***

A sting in Tamara's neck woke her. Her eyes flew open as a stimulant flowed into her bloodstream. The strap on her wrist jerked, and suddenly she was free. She acted instantly, twisting and struggling to reach the other strap, and freed her other arm. She sat up and released her legs then slid off the table and fell to the ground. A hand fell on her shoulder and she *peregrinated*.

A voice, a very familiar voice said from behind her, "If you let yourself be taken again, I'll have to kill you."

Tamara peered up, still on her knees. Her rescuer regarded Tamara with her own face and eyes, but now framed with bright red hair.

"Find your beloved doctor and a corner of the universe and hide." Her eyes—Tamara's eyes—were cold and devoid of emotion. "But if our brother takes you again, I will kill you to keep him from turning you into me." She disappeared, and Tamara collapsed on the floor of her twenty-first century Manhattan apartment. She was home.

***

Tamara didn't know how long she lay there on the kitchen floor, insensate, moaning, and filled with despair. She passed out a couple of times, and was delirious for part of the time, and she sensed that the sun set and rose again at least once. On the other hand, it could have been her imagination. Like the memory of the pain, and the enjoyment of the rape. A couple of times she found herself longing for a return to it, to the cycle of hurt and pleasure, and she hated herself for it.

"Tamara?"

"Danny!" She tried to sit up, but she lacked the strength.

He knelt and took her in his arms and held her, and she clung to him and wept. But when she awoke again he was gone, and she realized he'd only been there in her imagination. She lay on the kitchen floor and stared up at the ceiling, and did not care.

Nothing mattered anymore. Not her job. Not her Family. Not her people. Not her planet. Not Danny. She had nothing. She wanted nothing. She longed for nothing. A void had replaced her heart.

The angle of the sunlight slanting into the window shifted and then disappeared as time passed. The glow of day faded and darkened the window, gradually replaced by the neon and fluorescent glow of the city at night. Outside, horns honked, people called out, sirens came and went. And none of it meant anything to her.

She lay in the darkness and stared up at the shadows of the ceiling, and relived the eternity of torture. She could think of nothing else, as if she had never been rescued by—

Horror filled her again. Gods. Oh Gods. The *analogue*. She... I...

Tamara moaned. She remembered her own face and saw... madness. She had been broken. It... was broken. The creature constructed from her remains. Someone had taken her and broke her, and rebuilt *that* in her place.

Who are you? I don't know. The shadows around me may know, but not me.

The *analogue*. Tamara decided she had to kill her. She was broken and would do much harm. But... she was her. Someone had shattered her in order to recreate her. But who?

"Tamara! Get your ass up!" said Danny. Danny had never spoken to her in that tone, but he would, if he were here. No, he would be tender, and help her up, and hold her.

"Danny," she said, aloud this time, in a dry, hoarse whisper.

"Get up!" Danny insisted. "You aren't broken. Your nanites are repairing your body. You'll have your *ai* back soon. You need to get up and pull yourself together. You need to find me, Tamara."

Find me? She had to find *her* first. *Who am I? I am Tamara Decaire, daughter of Arran Decaire and Yana Cartine. I am a time-traveler and a Guardian of Time.*

"Arrogance!" says the mechanical voice of her captor. "Time needs no guardian. People do not need to be saved from their own folly. Your life has been wasted."

My life has been wasted.

"No," said her father's voice, a kind voice, even though he personally had killed thousands of people. "We committed an atrocity. Beran showed us how to repair our mistake. Then he convinced us to defend the innocent from megalomaniacs trying to change time. Your life has not been wasted, Tamara. You are a good person, and your life has been a good one."

His voice strengthened her. *I am Tamara. I am a good person, the daughter of a good man. I am hurt, but not lost. I am not lost.* For some reason, that phrase fortified her.

"I... am... not... lost...." She whispered aloud. "I... am not... lost." Her voice, her throat, her tongue was bone dry. There's water in the refrigerator. Get it.

She rolled onto her side. Her body was stiff and sore and didn't feel like her body at all. Of course not. The *analogue* had her body. That thought threatened to plunge her again into the darkness, but she stifled it. *I am Tamara. I am not lost.*

Her hands pressed against the cold tile floor and she pushed herself to her knees. She braced herself against the nearest cabinets as dizziness threatened to throw her back to the floor. Her sense of weakness angered her, and she clenched her teeth, grabbed the edge of the cabinets, and pulled herself to her feet. She leaned on the counter top, her legs trembling. She shuffled to the fridge and opened it, and the light made her flinch and slam the door shut.

Her heart pounded and she stared out the window into the night. Panic threatened to overwhelm her. Did someone see the light? Was her apartment under surveillance?

She couldn't be captured again.

She grabbed a large knife on the counter. She would kill herself before she let *him* take her again. She stared at the knife, gleaming darkly in the glow of city lights from the window. Perhaps that was the best answer. To die now. To remove the risk of being taken again. Without my *ai*, the failsafe would isolate me into a loop until someone from the Family came to save me. If anyone from the Family still lived. At least one did. My *analogue*.

But no. She's the real Tamara, older in the *natus* timeline. *I am the* analogue.

She blinked. Something trickled down her chest. She pulled the knife away and wiped at the blood, then touched the wound. It was a shallow cut. Her fingers were dark with blood splotches.

She shook her head, annoyed at herself. She set the knife down and opened the refrigerator again. She pulled out a bottle of water, opened, and drank. Emptied a second bottle. She wasn't hungry, but the nanites needed energy, so she pulled out a carton of eggs. She stepped over and turned on the kitchen light, ignoring the brief hammer of of disquiet that filled her.

When she finished eating, she stumbled to her bedroom. She was only half-aware that she sank to her hands and knees and crawled under her bed like a child, and fell asleep there.

Catena 2

Alea returned us to the cave complex on Vaerdine, after again pausing in the valley below Siola.

"You can't go directly to the cave?" I asked.

She shook her head. "Lerys set up a flux field to prevent direct *peregrinations*. This is the only portal with access."

Paul, Alea's twin, was conscious and waiting for us in the cavern, but when he saw me he frowned and began to talk to her in their odd, almost familiar language. I comprehended a few words this time, "home" and "burden" and I realized they were speaking a version of English a thousand years evolved from my time. And I gained the impression that Paul wanted to return me to my time because I was in their way.

"We need to find Tamara," I said, cutting them off. They stared at me. "What do we do next?"

Paul turned away muttering something vulgar and stamped toward the kitchen.

Alea had a troubled expression. "We need the rest of the Family here before we can act. Here we are safe."

"Which means Tamara isn't safe," I said. "Take me back to my time and I'll find her."

She took my hand. "You care for her. I saw it in your scan when you spoke of her. But Tamara is our best field agent. She knows how to go to ground when she needs to."

Her expression was open and sincere, and I could not sustain my glare.

"Come," she said, leading me down the middle corridor. It branched toward other rooms which I assumed were bedrooms or studies."

"How many live here?" I asked.

"Only Yana," she said. "But we all visit at times."

"Tell me about Yana."

"She was the chief medical officer for the misguided mission that brought our elders together. Now she is family doctor for all of us. She personally delivered all the second generation except for Tamara and Kyren."

"Why not them?"

"She gave birth to them," Alea said with a smile.

At the end of the corridor lay a large family room furnished with sofas, overstuffed chairs, a wine rack, and a fireplace. As they entered the room, the fireplace sprang to life with a whoosh.

"She's Tamara's mother?" I asked. "But she lives here alone?"

They pulled chairs close to the fire and sat. Then she stood again. "Wine?"

"Sure." The effects of the beer I'd had earlier had worn off, so I was glad for the offer.

She poured two glasses and brought one to me. She sat and began to sip. "Yana and Arran, Tamara's father, were together for the first few years. But they split and Yana moved in with Lerys for a time. Then she briefly reconciled with Arran. Then she moved here."

"Sounds like a lot of bad blood."

Alea fell silent. "Some. But time heals. Not to be ironic." She smiled. "That was more than a century and a half ago. We have all matured."

"So how many are there in the third generation?"

"None."

"None?"

"Doctor Beran had all of us sterilized when we were children."

That startled me. I considered the haggard hurt in her face. "Why?"

"He feared subsequent generations would lack the sense of... responsibility to our duty."

The tone of her voice when she said 'our duty' was poignant.

The reverberating bell sound indicating a new arrival shivered the air. Alea stood and took the wine glass from me and set it on the bar with hers.

I followed her to the portal chamber. Paul was already there. The new arrivals were Julian and a tall, striking dark-haired woman. She spoke to Paul and then to Alea in their exotic English. Both shook their heads. The new woman glared at Julian, but he also shook his head. She snapped at Alea, who sighed and stepped onto the platform as Julian stepped off. The two women disappeared, leaving me with Julian and Paul.

Paul gave us a dismissive glance and walked toward the kitchen area.

Julian regarded me, held out his hand. "I seek forgiveness for my earlier actions. It is a difficult time for us."

He smiled, and his smile made him appear even younger and prettier than he already did. I accepted his hand and nodded. Julian's grip was firm, and his smile engaging. "Welcome, then, Danny. Alea has no doubt vetted you, so I trust you. You must forgive Paul, though. He is the angriest of us." He placed a companionable arm on my shoulders and led me toward the great room.

"Why is he angry?" I asked.

Julian chuckled and said in his strange accent, "He is Lerys' son. Emotional, judgmental, and reactionary. Traits to make him a formidable soldier and an abysmal diplomat."

"And you are his brother."

A shadow crossed Julian's dark eyes and he removed his arm from my shoulder. "Half-brother. We share a mother, Paul, Alea, and I: the valiant Sheyn Liann." There was a strange undercurrent in his voice that made me glance at his face. Julian's lips thinned. "Sheyn achieved a singular status amongst our *Family*. She has been the only one of us to die."

A pang of sympathy touched Danny's chest. "I'm sorry."

Julian's set expression did not change.

They entered the great room and Julian stepped to the wet bar. He opened an elegant crystal decanter filled with amber liquid and poured himself a drink with no ice and no mixer. He downed it in one motion, and poured a second. He glanced at me with a question but I shook my head and retrieved my wine. Julian sat in the chair Alea had vacated, and I joined him. The aroma of Julian's drink was potent, and I wondered if I should have one after all.

Julian regarded me with his dark eyes, a strange contrast to his fair complexion. He said, "I learned about you, when I was there looking for Tamara."

"Oh?"

"You are well regarded by your peers and coworkers," he said. "The best doctor they know."

In spite of myself, that bestowed a warm thrill. I wasn't expecting compliments from him.

Julian said, "You would make a great addition to our Family."

My heart skipped a beat. In the back of my mind, ever since I accepted that Tamara had been telling the truth, a part of me had yearned to be a part of her reality. I'd had a glimpse of the future and I wanted to embrace it and never let go. And now Julian was almost offering me a place here. I wanted it desperately.

I said, trying to sound modest, "There is so much I would have to learn about modern medicine."

Julian smiled and took a drink.

The arrival bell sounded.

Julian said, "That will be the girls returning with Lor."

Steps echoed down the corridor. The tall woman entered the room arm-in-arm with a dark, dour, lanky man with a pronounced adam's apple and thick, black brows and short straight hair. He didn't wear glasses, but he seemed like he ought to. He stopped when he saw me.

"Who are you?"

He spoke in their exotic language, but this time I understood both the words and the context.

"Danny Nolan," Alea said from behind him. "Tamara's *inamorato*."

I wanted to correct her, but I did not look away from the cold unfriendliness in Lor's dark eyes. I felt vulnerable sitting down so I stood to face him. I was taller by several inches. Lor noted it and glowered.

"I was not aware," he said, "it is now our policy to bring home our paramours."

"There is much of which you are unaware," said Paul's equally cold voice as he reached Alea's side.

Lor's eyes narrowed at the sound of Paul's voice, but he did not break contact with me. "And who are you, Danny Nolan?"

I said, "I'm a doctor." I felt obligated to clarify: "A resident."

"From?" Lor asked.

I hesitated, uncertain of how to answer. "From twenty-first century Earth."

"Ah," Lor said. "Tamara's favorite era." He stepped closer to me, peering at me as if looking for some physical flaw. "Early or late?"

"Early," I said. "Twenty-fourteen."

Lor said, "The final decades of the pre-Raslan era." He paused a moment, his eyes flicking back and forth in an odd way. "Bet on Seattle in the Super Bowl."

"Stop it, Lor," Alea said.

"Why? Who doesn't like conversations with fossils?"

"By giving him information about his future?"

"I'm sorry," Lor said. "Was he under the impression we would ever let him return to his time?"

A coldness settled into my gut. But before I could say anything, the tall, beautiful woman still holding Lor's arm spoke.

"Lor. Go fix me a drink, sweetie." Her tone could not be ignored.

"As you wish, dear Kyren," said Lor, nodding to me and then to her. He stepped over to the bar, leaving Kyren to beam at me. She stepped to me and kissed me soundly on the lips. She tasted and smelled of an exotic fruit.

"Tamara chose well," she said with a mischievous smile, sweeping his form with her blue-grey eyes. "If you ever grow tired of her, you know where to find me." She winked at me, and I had the impression she wasn't being entirely facetious.

"We're here," Paul said loudly, glaring at her. "Everyone be seated."

"And naturally you assume you are in charge?" Lor said, still at the bar.

"I am," Paul said, straightening his shoulders and placing his hands on his hips. He wore a gun on his belt, with a cobalt blue grip.

Alea noticed the gun and caught her breath. "You won't need that, Paul!"

"Lerys is missing," Paul said. "That makes me Master at Arms."

"Missing," Lor said. He brought Kyren her drink. "Not dead." He pulled a chair up for her and a second for himself. "Which makes you, officially, nothing."

Paul's jaw tightened along the line of his beard.

"And Lor is eldest," Kyren said. "Which means he should conduct this meeting."

"Eldest *child*!" Paul snapped. "Our parents are missing!"

"We are not children," Julian said. He had not turned his chair around to face the others. He stared into the fire.

Paul drew a deep breath. "Yes. You are correct, Julian. Lor, please brief us on the Shen."

I retook my seat.

Lor sipped from his crystal tumbler. "They have not reached fruition. I estimate another two years before any further intervention is required."

"Could they be aware of us?" Alea asked. "Could they be behind these attacks?"

"I said they have not reached fruition," Lor said.

"Could they reach fruition without you knowing it?" Julian asked.

Lor glared at him, but Julian continued to gaze into the fire.

Kyren said, "We all have *sirdar* links to warn us if the *natus* timeline has been changed. We would know."

I wasn't sure what she meant by *sirdar*, though I did sense that she was speaking up to defend Lor. But something occurred to me. I said, "You can *peregrinate* without changing the *natus* timeline. You people do it constantly. Do you have

80

something that detects simple movement through time?" He glanced at Julian then at Alea. He realized they were all staring at him. Alea and Julian were both smiling, but Paul and Lor glared at him.

"No, we don't," Kyren said, looking to Lor for confirmation.

His lips thinned and he shook his head.

"You are suggesting," said Alea, "that the Shen have indeed secretly reached fruition but have refrained from changing the *natus* timeline to avoid alerting us."

"Is it possible?" I asked Julian, who shrugged and looked at Lor.

"Yes," Lor said. "It is possible. But not likely. My father and I have been watching them."

"And he is gone with the rest," said Paul without a trace of sympathy.

Lor seemed about to surge to his feet, but Kyren placed her hand on his arm.

"Who else is capable of attacking us?" Alea said to distract Lor. He relaxed and turned thoughtful.

"The Alphans have the capability," he said. "And of course the Keyerans."

Julian sniffed. "Perhaps Beran has reconciled with his people and is now helping them."

"Silence, Julian," Kyren said. "Beran is your father as well as Lor's, and we know his loyalty is to us, not to the Keyerans."

"Well…" Paul said. "If not Beran, perhaps Andresen? Maybe he is secretly aiding the Alosians?" No one rose to defend Andresen, whoever he was, but no one seemed to take the idea seriously either. For a long moment, everyone was lost in thought.

The arrival bell rang and they exchanged expressions of surprise and turned to the corridor.

Tamara entered the room and my heart leapt to see her. I jumped up and went to her. When she saw me, her expression changed to relief and she surged forward hug me.

"Tamara!" Alea exclaimed.

Tamara's momentum made us both stumble, and we bumped into Paul.

"What happened--" Lor began, then stopped when he saw Paul's blue-handled pistol in Tamara's hand.

Tamara pushed me behind her and began to back away from the rest.

"What the hell!" Paul snapped.

"Tam?" Julian said, shock on his face.

"Be still!" Tamara said. "All of you." She backed farther, directing me through the corridor. I was so surprised by her action that I let her guide me. "You have a problem, Brothers and Sisters. One of you has betrayed us. You need to find out who it is and stop them. I only know it isn't me, so I am going to take Danny and disappear."

I moved down the corridor and Tamara followed, watching behind her; but none of her family pursued. We climbed onto the platform. I grimaced in anticipation of the *peregrination*, and we were in the valley. Tamara took my hand and my world reeled again and cold air swirled around us.

We stood in front of a small, secluded cabin nestled in snowdrifts and surrounded by snow-covered fir trees. Off to my left rose distant grey-white mountains, and to my right lay a broad field of snow that sloped down to a small brook and then back up to a far-away tree line. In two remote areas in the field of white, steam drifted from the ground, filling the air above with pallid clouds. Quiet and solitude as palpable as a woolen blanket covered the area.

I realized Tamara was watching me and not smiling. "Are you all right?" I asked.

She nodded, but uncertainty clouded her face.

"What's wrong?" I asked.

She bit her lip. "Are *you* all right?" she said.

"Yeah," I said. "Yeah. It's a lot to take in, but I'm good. And cold! Is that for us?" I indicated the cabin.

She nodded, and we crunched and struggled through the snow to the steps and climbed to the porch. A pair of rocking chairs and a wooden swing occupied the area in front of the cabin. I stamped the snow off his sneakers, but my blue scrub pants were soaked and my ankles were turning to ice.

The warmth inside embraced me and I sighed. A fire burned in an antique wood-burning stove in the corner farthest from the door. I stepped to it, holding out my numb hands to warm them. Tamara took a blanket and threw it over my shoulders. She put her arms around me and pressed her cheek against my shoulder.

"I'm glad you're okay," she said. "I was afraid--"

I took her hands. Her fingers were ice cold. There were no stitches on her hands or arms, no scars either. I turned, holding her hands to look at them. The wounds were all gone. I looked up to her haunted eyes. "How long?"

Her dark eyes held a troubled cast I had never seen before. "Too long," she said. I gazed at her until she said, "A year."

Despite all I knew now, that shook me. Only a few hours had passed for me. She was a different person now than the wounded woman who had come to my emergency room. But now she seemed more frightened than ever. "What's wrong?" I asked.

She shook her head and her gaze fell.

"Tamara! What's wrong?"

"Nothing," she said. "Are you hungry? I will prepare you something." She tried to pull away, but I held on to her hands. She violently wrenched them out of me grasp and glared at me. "Don't ever do that again."

I drew away from the venom in her voice, startled.

She held my gaze for a moment, then her eyes lost focus and she disappeared.

I gaped at the spot. Damn! Did she mean to do that, or had something happened to her? I didn't know enough about their technology to know if they could find and attack someone without ever coming to this space-time.

She returned an hour later in a cheerful mood carrying paper bags with the logo of an Italian restaurant. "I've decided we're having spaghetti." She produced two plastic containers and forks, and sat with me on the sofa, which faced a large window looking out over the winter vista.

When I smelled the food I realized I was starving, and joined her in devouring the food. Halfway through the meal I remembered something and stopped. "Alea injected me with nanites."

Tamara nodded and continued to eat.

The food turned to lead in my stomach as I thought it through. "What are they doing to me?"

"Healing you."

"I'm not hurt."

"Repairing you."

"Repairing what?"

"The natural aging process, for one thing."

I stared at her. "How long will they be… inside me?"

"You won't need another injection. They're self-replicating."

"So I am permanently infected? With miniature robots?" The idea nauseated me. I was still hungry, but couldn't eat anymore.

Tamara saw my discomfort. She took my food and hers and set them aside on an end table. Then she leaned into me and said, "Hold me."

I wrapped my arm around her and she laid her head on my chest, and I let her soft warmth distract me. We gazed through the window at the winter landscape.

"I'm glad my family found you," Tamara said, her voice muffled by my shirt. "So do you believe me now?"

The memory of her shooting flechettes into the floor made me chuckle. "Yes. You were persuasive. Well... actually your sister was. Very pretty too. Does she have a boyfriend?"

Tamara gasped and pounded her fist into my gut and I grunted and laughed.

"Are you okay?" she asked, peering into my face with an unusual solemnity. "With everything?"

"It's a little overwhelming," I said, gazing into her brown eyes and appealing face.

I frowned. A scar, mostly healed but still there, faint, run under her right eye. It had not been there before; the last time he'd seen her in the hotel room. He reached up to touch it lightly. "What happened to you?"

Her expression clouded and she sat up, and he felt the loss of her closeness. "Nothing," she said. "Nothing important."

"Tamara," I said.

She stood and gathered up the trash and stuffed it into the paper sacks. Tears glinted on her face from the light slowing in from the window.

I stood and intercepted her and caught her shoulders. Her face was tortured. I took her in my arms and held her. She resisted at first, then she clung to me. She was trembling. I led her to the sofa and sat her down.

"Tell me," I said gently.

"He found me," she said, her voice quavering.

"Who?"

She didn't answer immediately. "One of my brothers. I think. He tortured me."

I hugged her. "I'm so sorry, hon." I held her as she shook. She clung to me and wept.

After a time her tears stopped and she lay recumbent in my arms. I stroked her shoulder with my fingertips. When she began to snore softly, I smiled down at her.

Catena 1

Tamara screamed and moaned and suffered from the pain of torture, from the humiliation-guilt-enjoyment of rape, from the horror of seeing her analogue and realizing that she was--in reality--the duplicate. Then she dreamed of loneliness, lost in a dark maze, with only an indistinct shadow at times pursuing her and at other times seeming to lead her.

She awoke to an intermittent thump. She was lying on the sofa. Outside, the day had darkened toward twilight. The snow covered trees and fields were in shadow, and the sky had a pale glow. The thump sounded again. From outside.

Tamara bolted upright and the blanket covering her fell away. She shivered and pulled it back up and wrapped it around her shoulders. The thump sounded again. She stood up and went to the window.

Danny was using a maul to split wood. He wore the jeans and flannel shirt she'd bought for him but had not had the opportunity to present to him. She had spent months preparing this hideout, stocking it with the supplies she thought they would need.

She watched him work, watching the form of his arms and torso, the sheen of perspiration on his face, the tousle of his blond hair by the wind. She gazed at him and his raw strength, and the aura of reliability he radiated. She felt safer just seeing him. He paused, wiped his brow with his arm, then saw her and smiled. Her heart jumped at that simple smile and she returned it without conscious thought.

It took him three trips to bring in the wood he'd split and deposit it in the bin near the stove.

"Are you feeling better?" he asked.

Tamara nodded.

He crouched in front of the stove and added a couple pieces of wood, and adjusted the damper. "Are you warm enough?"

She nodded again. But it was possible she would have nodded no matter what she felt.

He stepped to the collection of cardboard boxes in the corner, opened one, and pulled out a box of wine and two plastic cups. The way he moved suggested he'd already opened them and knew what was there. He poured the wine and handed her one, then sat on the sofa and set the wine box on the end table. She sat with him. His smell was strong and musky, but not at all unpleasant. She leaned into him and he put his arm around her. He was warm after his exertions, and she basked in his glow.

"Do you feel up to talking?" he asked.

She didn't, but she nodded. He deserved answers.

"You think one of your brothers did this?"

"I never saw who had me, and his voice was masked. But it... *felt* familiar. But not enough for me to identify it."

"And you believe he is responsible for your parents as well?"

"Yes." She had sought out her father after she was able to *peregrinate* again. When she found him gone, she searched for the others. "It had to be someone capable of doing what we do, and who knew where to find each of them. Beran was right."

"About what?"

"He believed that with each generation, the chances would rise that one of us would be a sociopath, someone with fantastic capabilities and no conscience."

"That's why he had you sterilized."

"Alea told you? She is the one most distressed by that. She has long wanted children and begged our parents to reverse the sterilization for her."

"I sensed that Beran's policies are contentious."

Tamara sniffed. "Beran's policies *are* the contention. Some want to stick with them, some want to discard them-- and Beran's leadership--entirely."

"Paul and Julian are clearly anti-Beran," Danny said. "Probably Alea too, from what you said. Lor is pro. Kyren defended Lor and thus Beran indirectly. Which faction do you belong to?"

"I support him," Tamara said. "He is a genius; the smartest man I have ever met. He founded our Family and has led it for over two hundred years. My father trusts him, and so do I."

"Tell me about your father."

She remembered the last time going to her father's cabin on prehistoric Lethiel. He loved the natural world and had instilled that love in her. The place had been deserted. "Arran Decaire. He was the demolitions expert for the team that originally tried to win a war by altering history. He stood with Beran when they resolved to keep anyone from

90

manipulating time again. All of them agreed at the start. My father wasn't a scientist, but he knew his field. He, Lerys, and Sheyn trained us. Physical training, endurance, hand-to-hand combat, shooting of just about every firearm ever invented. Explosives. Electronics. Espionage."

"You are beautiful *and* deadly," Danny said with a wink as he refilled our wine cups. "You can't beat that." His words warmed her and she grinned at him.

Then he was kissing her. Lightly and softly at first, his lips tasting mine. She leaned in and his arm tightened around her, and her lips parted for him. He must've set his cup down, because his hand was now free and touched her face, caressing her cheek and neck.

She lost herself in the moment, enjoying his taste, his smell, and his touch. It had been a long time since someone kissed her like this.

Unwanted memories seeped into her mind like a toxin, the wet taste and stale odor of her captor, the weight of his body, the pain of his beatings and of the ice-cold table.

Catena 2

I sensed the change in her. She went stiff and turned her face from me. He released her and sat back. Her eyes were closed and her face extraordinarily pale. Her jaw was clenched, and her lips pressed together. She grimaced as if she was in pain and her hands curled into fists. I touched her hand but she jerked it away.

"Don't touch me!" she said without opening her eyes.

I watched her. Slowly color returned to her face, but it was the flush of embarrassment. Or anger. Her eyes fluttered opened. They were filled with unshed tears.

"Tamara. What's wrong? Are you hurt?"

She smiled slightly. "Always the doctor," she murmured.

I brushed a strand of hair from her face. "What's wrong, hon?"

She bit her lower lip and a tear fell from her eye. "You are so kind," she whispered. "I don't deserve you."

I took her hand and this time she did not pull away. "Tell me what happened."

"He broke me." Her voice caught.

I squeezed her hand. "It's over now, hon."

"No. He broke me. Like a horse is broken. So he could use me. He broke me and owns me now."

I regarded her uncertainly. I wasn't sure what she meant, but it sounded ominous. And it filled me with fury. How could someone do that to this woman, strong and beautiful and steadfast, who had spent her entire life performing a duty someone else had chosen for her?

"No," I said, groping for words to comfort her. "No one owns you. And I intend to break the man who tried to break you."

She smiled sadly and reached up to touch my cheek. "A knight in shining armor," she said quietly. "I thought you were a myth."

I took her hand and kissed it. But she withdrew it and stood.

"Listen, Danny. I need you to understand this." She held my gaze. "I am not the real Tamara. *He* has the real one."

Disquiet filled me. I tried to keep it from my expression, but I couldn't. Had she really been psychologically broken? I studied her, examining her for signs of psychosis.

But my expression angered her and she slapped me. The blow shook me emotionally. I never expected that kind of attack from her. I couldn't suppress the expression of real hurt on my face, but that only angered her more.

"Listen to me! Without your caveman prejudices! I told you about our most important stricture. We do what we can--we do what we *must*--to avoid changing our own *catenae*. Otherwise we create an *analogue*. It's as if I suddenly had an identical twin, but worse, because her memories and feelings and every single thing about her is *Me*."

I realized what she was trying to say. With a sick feeling I said, "You... are not..."

Tears began to stream down her face. "I am! I am the one you saved. The one you held and watched over in the motel room. The one who wants to kiss you, and hold you, and just be with you! And I am the one you want to kiss, the one you want to touch, the one you want to fuck! *And so is she!*" She tried to scream the last part, but her voice broke. She turned away from me and buried her face in trembling hands.

I stood and put my hands on her shoulder, but she stepped away. I understood her turmoil now. Two of her, equal in every way. Then which one am I attracted to? Which one did I long to kiss? Even if they were the same from his perspective, from their perspective they were now different, and now struggling with a profound identity crisis.

"Tell me about... the other one," I said.

She didn't meet my gaze. "I... couldn't get away. I was bound, and blindfolded. Until she freed me and brought me home. And she said if I was captured again, she would kill me to keep me from being turned into... her."

My throat tightened. Somewhere--*somewhen*--someone had taken Tamara, his Tamara, and turned her into a psychopath. They had turned her into something so terrible that she had broken a cardinal rule of her people and changed her own timeline. And she was still out there. The Tamara whom I had fallen so hard for. I could understand this Tamara's turmoil better now.

This Tamara? But this was also my Tamara. She had doubts, though, and those doubts were eating at her.

"I am an *analogue*," she said, still not facing me. "She is the real Tamara, because she has the older *catena*. I am just her creation." She glared at me. "She is the one you want!"

I didn't know what to say. I didn't know how to reassure her. Reassure her of what? That I desired her? That he wanted *her*, not her other self?

"You are completely as real as she is," I said. "You are Tamara. *My* Tamara." She regarded me doubtfully. I took her face between my hands, brushed her tears away with my thumbs as I gazed into her bright eyes.

I kissed her, long, deeply, passionately, tasting the saltiness of her tears and the tang of the wine. She moaned and leaned into me, wrapping her arms around me, pressing the length of her body against mine. My kisses moved down to her neck and my fingers curled through her hair

"Please don't leave me," she whispered. "I couldn't bear it if you left."

"I won't leave you," I said, my voice gruff. I kissed her mouth again, so long and hard it left us breathless. Our tongues and lips danced together as we inhaled each other's breaths. My hands fell to her hips and pressed her against me hard, and her hands caressed my arms and back.

For long into the night, time had no meaning for us.

Catena 3

Tamara Prime had to take Lerys first. He was the stern soldier, the hardcore drill sergeant, and the one most capable of opposing the rebels.

And he was the one she had to be most careful with. She was a better fighter than he was now, and smarter, but he was wily and tough. The irony was he sympathized with the rebels, those who wanted to do away with Beran's arrangement. But he would never act against his comrades. He was too loyal for that.

Lerys lived on his home planet, Lethiel, the tidal-locked twin of Vaerdine; the two planets spun around each other as they orbited the Alosian sun. Tamara arrived and looked up as she always did, to see the huge, hazy crescent of Vaerdine taking up a third of the bright blue sky. The sun, a tiny, white-hot orb burned fiercely just above the eastern horizon, but the wind swirling around her was bitter. The landscape around Lerys' home was barren, rocky, and snow-covered. She shuddered, remembering the nights alone in that harsh land, learning to survive on her own wits and determination.

To her right rose a pyramid-shaped structure half embedded in the hilltop, made of a material that appeared like simple red mud brick covered with a layer of ice. But it had actually been grown organically and contained a myriad of circuits and switches to change its color to blend into its surroundings, even to turn the house invisible if necessary.

Lerys used to share his home with Sheyn, the mother of his two children, the twins Alea and Paul--until she'd left him and their irreconcilable differences. Her death had struck Lerys hard, and had made him even more withdrawn, inflexible, and focused on his work.

Lerys' home was an armory of ancient and modern weapons. He'd trained the children in all of them, from swords and spears, to muskets, to plasma blasters. When she passed through the triangle shaped doorway, a chime sounded to announce her arrival.

The house was pristine and sparse except for the weapons displayed on every wall. Lerys wasn't in the kitchen or living room, so she knew where he would be. She descended to the basement levels where he'd built a series of shooting ranges, training simulators, and a gym.

Tamara walked down the corridor, remembering the times she'd come here for training. This had been a second home for her. She loved Lerys like a father, and feared him a little for the stern taskmaster he was. But now only her mission mattered.

She heard explosions and followed them down the corridor. Sonic, she thought; a *lei qiang*. He was practicing with a Shen weapon. She entered the observation room and stepped to the window.

Master Sergeant Lerys Eril was a short, broad-shouldered man with crew-cut iron-grey hair and a neat, equally grey goatee. He wore a Shen dragon suit, a chameleon-like jump suit that changed colors and blended in with its surrounding. Tamara began to rework her plan, because that dragon suit was also projectile proof and energy resistant, and would turn aside the charge of her stun gun.

Lerys tumbled and rolled to his feet and shot his gun at the holographic image that stepped from behind a wall, then tumbled again as it returned fire. The weapon he carried discharged tight pellets of sonic energy that acted like explosive bullets. Messy and harrowing against flesh and blood targets, which is one reason the Shen used them. Lerys was modeling a Shen attack on a Vaerdine station. And he was playing the Shen this time. He'd often said the best way to fight an enemy was to understand him, and see the fight from his eyes.

He scanned ahead for targets she could not see, because the impulses were being generated by his *ai*. To him they were real images, and his *ai* would react accordingly if he were shot, generating the pain and disorientation of a real wound.

Hmmm. She could use that. She used her own *ai* to access the simulation.

Catena 4

Lerys Eril was an old man. Physically, he had never been in better condition. But mentally? Spiritually? In his youth, a teenager enduring the basic training of the Alosian Defense Force, he'd not only believed himself invulnerable, he'd felt like he would indeed live forever. Lerys had risen to the rank of Master Sergeant in the ADF, and then was chosen for the fateful mission that changed his life forever. The mission had cost him the woman he loved, and cost him his home, but it had given him a new life and a new purpose. And a new family.

He had not known any of the other surviving members of the expedition, but he had supported Beran completely, and he had grown to care for the other members of this new, extended family he found himself in. And especially he had grown to love the children he'd watched grow up, youths he'd trained with a rigor greater than he'd ever experienced in boot camp, honing them into perfect warriors to best even the Shen dragon soldiers.

But, now, he had grown weary of the constant conflict, the ceaseless vigilance. A vigilance with no respite and no end in sight, and no one to eventually pass the responsibility to. Beren had forbidden any further offspring. So there were twelve (eleven now) people to stand watch over Time, and do it forever?

In his youth, Lerys had considered immortality an alluring possibility. But now? After three hundred years of this? Lerys had read once that the greatest fear of any immortal being would have to be that they would, indeed, live forever. He didn't understand that then.

It wasn't that he disliked his role as the gruff drill sergeant. It wasn't that he disliked any of other Family members. And it wasn't that he disapproved of the burden the Family had taken upon itself. It was just that, since Sheyn's very real death, Lerys had found within himself a festering emptiness, a sadness, a sense of futility that poisoned his sense of optimism of a future where anything was possible. He found himself, from time to time, wondering what it would really be like to die.

Some spiritualists still believed in a soul, a singularity of personal, individual energy that somehow managed to survive the death of the body and... what? There was no consensus on what happened after death. Some thought the energy of the soul merged with a universal consciousness, a kind of dynamic field from which all the other fields arose, giving the universe itself sentience. There were also the afterlives of conventional religion, all sounding either absurd of excruciatingly boring.

Lerys had always been a hard-headed empiricist. No proof, no evidence, then no belief. It had served him well in his life. Except, now he had begun to wonder what was really out there, on the other side. Probably nothing. But he did wonder.

So he spent most of his time throwing himself into his duties as the instructor, and also his avocation as an advisor to the ADF military. The Family did not take sides in the political conflicts going on around them, but Lerys could and did help the people who had been *his* people. As long as Lerys did not touch the timeline, Beran had acquiesced. So Lerys had been studying the tactics of the Shen. Their ruthless eugenics had produced soldiers of inimitable prowess: dog soldiers to scout, tiger soldiers with suprahuman strength and agility armed with killing claws on their hands, and finally the dragon soldiers, elite warriors of superior skill, intelligence, and toughness.

The attack would start with a punch, a needle ship slamming through the EM shield and into the station. Out would pour tiger soldiers to sweep away any defenders. Then the dragon soldiers would come, armed with dragon suits and *lei qiangs* to finalize the takeover.

He ordered the dragon soldiers to attack the command center. He knew the Alosian soldiers that were part of the simulation were tasked to destroy the station should they decide all was lost, so the assault had to be swift. The soldiers staggered as clouds of flechettes struck them, but the material of the suits were designed to withstand the darts.

A beanbag projectile struck Lerys in the chest and exploded in a cloud of white powder. *What the hell?* He rolled away, but the powder clung to him like a paste and his suit began to fall off in globs like wet paint. Shit. A flash-bang grenade went off near him, causing him to stagger. Another grenade began to emit a barely audible but painful shriek that would incapacitate with disorientation and vomiting.

Lerys located the sonic grenade and blasted it, and the sound ceased. But nearly half of his dragon suit had dissolved now. A dozen tiny holes appeared in his chest and he fell back as agony filled him. It wasn't real, but his *ai* fed him impulses as if it were. He couldn't breathe, and tasted the copper tang of blood in his mouth. The blood filled his throat and he gurgled helplessly.

He triggered his failsafe and peregrinated to the control room.

"Hmph!" he grunted. "I knew someone was fuckin' with the program when the *orthocarboran* pouch hit me." He frowned at Tamara, his version of a smile. He was happy to see her. She'd always been his best student. "Good idea, though. I'll pass that on to the VDF." His eyes raked me. "You here for training, I hope. You look soft."

"Soft?" Tamara said, rising to his bait. "I'm never soft!"

"Too soft," he rumbled, amused. "You been taking it easy. And that red hair is just plain ugly." He frowned at her. "Are you okay? You keep clenching your fists."

She stilled her hands, giving him a strange, unreadable look. She drew the stun pistol from her belt and aimed it at him. His iron-grey brow only rose fractionally.

She shot him.

Catena 3

The blue electric bolt struck him in the chest and dissipated, but all he did was gaze at Tamara with an unreadable expression.

"So," he said. "It has finally come."

She stared at him with growing dread. The stun gun should have worked. It could disable any one of them, but it didn't touch him.

She backed toward the door, but still he just watched her.

Lerys sighed. "I am sorry, Tamara. I had expected Paul to be the one, but it was wise to choose you. You were always my best soldier."

She tried to keep the dismay from her face. "You knew?"

He said, "Beran predicted it a hundred years ago, that our children would rise against us eventually."

That shook her. Beran knew? Which meant all the Elders knew. That changed everything. "But... you trained us."

"I trained you damn well!" Lerys barked, his voice gruff. "Perhaps well enough that you will win. If so, you will make me proud of you." His eyes were bright.

Tamara pressed her back to the wall, frightened and at a loss. She almost turned and ran. But she couldn't. Julian would kill her if she did. Fool. He's getting into her head. Her mouth was dry, but she said, "Will you not join us, Uncle?"

Lerys sighed. "You know I can't, Tammy." He stepped toward her and her heart began to beat faster. He looked sad. "You do understand you must kill me."

That rattled her. "We aren't planning on killing anyone!"

He smiled sadly. "Still the sweet little girl. You must, though. Otherwise your little uprising doesn't stand a chance. I would stop it in its tracks." He seemed honestly apologetic about that, as if he would have preferred that their uprising succeed. A blue-handled stun pistol like her own appeared in his hand.

She dodged without waiting to see if he aimed. An electric snap loud enough to make her ears ring burst out, and a scorch mark appeared on the wall where she'd been as she tumbled out the door into the corridor.

As she rolled, she drew her flechette gun. Julian had reprogrammed it to imbue the darts with a neurotoxin. She slid to a stop and shot behind her without aiming. The darts plinked off the walls. She waited, but he didn't show himself. She jumped up and investigated the room, but he was gone.

Impossible! Lerys' house was surrounded by a flux field that prevented *peregrination*. She tried it now, just to assure herself that she could not jump; but something in Lerys' *ai* or in the setting of the field allowed him to do things the rest of the Family could not. That was an important piece of information. It meant she had to render him unconscious, because otherwise he would be able to jump away if wounded, and his fail-safe would activate if she killed him quickly.

She dashed through the corridors and into the living room and grabbed a dagger from the wall. She crouched between the sofa and the wall. Another flash and snap of electricity arced over her head and into the wall behind her. She was about to peer over the sofa to get a range on him when she changed her mind and tumbled away instead. With the sound of ripping fabric and impacts, holes appeared in the sofa and in the wall at the spot where she'd been.

She fell from behind the sofa and threw her dagger. It slammed into his abdomen and he grunted. He adjusted his aim and the railgun in his hand snapped and more holes appeared in the floor and wall where she'd been, hurling debris and dust into the air.

"First blood!" he called out, and his voice was--to her disbelief--proud. "I knew I trained you well!"

She continued to tumble. That railgun would go through just about anything. Then it occurred to her that he wasn't trying to kill her so much as push her in the direction he wanted her to go, so she arrested her momentum and fell on her back. A concussive blast erupted in the kitchen, where she been headed.

She aimed in the direction where he'd been standing. Her gun snapped multiple times and a spread of holes appeared in the sofa. Lerys gasped.

She dared to peek over the edge. Lerys held his bleeding left arm to his chest. But he was aiming the heavy railgun again with just his right hand, holding it steady in a show of prodigious strength.

She dived away and the sofa shattered into debris. She charged around the perimeter, and he couldn't move the gun quickly enough to draw a bead on her. He continued to fire, though, and holes exploded in the walls behind her.

She rolled toward him, kicked out and swept his legs from under him. He fell, dropping the gun, but he returned to his feet as quickly as she did. She began to strike him, moving constantly to his left. His bleeding left arm moved a trifle slower, and she was able to land a few good blows.

She struck his chest and he staggered, but it was a feint. She followed, but he ducked under her blow and wrapped his powerful arms around her. She struck him twice in the head with blows that would have dropped any other man, but he lifted her up and slammed her back and head against his crystal coffee table. Pain exploded through her. She might have lost consciousness for a moment, but suddenly he had her on the floor in a chokehold. She struggled, but he held her in a position where she could not get leverage.

"You should not have closed with me, Tammy," Lerys said in her ear.

"Still... teaching... uncle," she gasped. He tightened his grip and her vision went hazy. She let herself go limp. To her surprise, he eased his hold and rolled her off him with unexpected gentleness.

When he sat up, so did she. They gazed at each other. He climbed to his feet and held out his good arm. She took his powerful hand and he pulled her up.

He said, "Did I hurt you?"

She almost laughed at that. "Not really. I hurt you though."

"Eh," he waved dismissively.

"We need to get you to Yana."

"For these gnat bites?"

"Uncle, the flechettes were poisoned."

He smiled sadly. "Ah, Tammy. Didn't I tell you that you would have to kill me?"

Unbidden, tears filled her eyes. "No. We'll go to Yana

"You gonna carry me?"

The tears trickled down her face. "If necessary."

He shook his head, still smiling, and started for the stairs leading down to the training rooms. "I guess you won after all."

"No!" Tamara snapped. "You can't quit now. You have a duty to protect your team."

He paused, and put his hand on the wall. "My team," he murmured. He sagged to his knees.

"Uncle!" She dashed to his side, put her hand on his shoulder. She tried to *peregrinate* to Vaerdine, but she couldn't. He put his back to the wall and slid to the floor with a sigh. Tamara stood over him with her hands on my hips, glaring.

"Spare me the lecture, girl," Lerys said, his chest heaving with effort to breathe. "You have poisoned me, and now you want to go to Yana, and use me as a distraction so you can kill her as well."

"Why would I kill my own mother!" she shouted. His accusation shook her because she had planned exactly that. Not the killing part, but all the rest.

She took his arm and tried to drag him toward the door. He was growing weaker, but not too weak to resist her. He pulled away, nearly making her fall. She would have to wait until he passed out.

But he glared at her. "You will leave me here or I'll jump somewhere you won't find me to die alone. I don't... want to die alone."

Now the tears flowed freely down her face. She crouched next to him. "Why do you want to die, Uncle?"

"Tired," Lerys said, his chest heaving with an effort to breathe. "Three hundred years. And I love... the kids."

She took his hand and wept as Lerys Eril lost his struggle for breath. His heaving chest fell still and his eyes closed and he sagged against her, and her tears fell on his grey hair.

Catena 2

I woke and reached for Tamara but she wasn't there. The door of the cast iron stove closed in the front room. She must have just put another log in. I also smelled coffee brewing.

I stretched my long legs in the bed languorously and smiled. She was an amazing woman, strong, self-reliant, and passionate. She was no damsel in distress who needed me to do anything for her. If she were cold, she would add wood to the fire. If she were hungry, she would eat.

Orange morning sunlight slanted into the window. Had it only been two days since she had convinced me to help her escape the hospital? How did a time traveler measure time? For me it had been two days, but for her it had been a year. A year of torture and rape.

My smile faded. Tamara had suffered. She still suffered. I could see it in her eyes and her expressions when she was less guarded. And one of her brothers had done it to her.

She came in carrying two steaming mugs of coffee. She smiled when she saw I was awake. She wore a short, pink robe that fell just barely to her thighs, leaving her long, brown legs bare. God she was sexy.

I accepted the mug from her and set it on the side table as she sat with me. I deliberately took her mug and set it on the table as well, then proceeded to remove her robe.

She giggled, then sighed when I kissed her exposed flesh. She pulled me down to her.

After a period of expended energy, we ended up with arms and limbs entwined, breathing hard. She lay against my chest, her leg and arm thrown over me, her head on my shoulder.

"I want to stay here," she said, her warm breath brushing his chest. "With you. Forever."

"I do too," I said.

She raised her head. "Do you?" Her dark eyes were vulnerable and haunted now.

"I do," I said with a sincerity that surprised me.

"I wish..." she bit her lip and laid her head down so I could not see her face.

"What do you wish?"

"That I could believe you."

That surprised and hurt me.

She said, "I can't trust anyone."

"You can trust me," I said.

She didn't respond. Something tickled my chest; her tears.

"I'm afraid," she said. "I'm an *analogue*. I'm not the *real* me. My family will reject me. A part of me wants to never return to them. But I must."

"You are real," I said. "Absolutely. Unequivocally. Real in every sense of the word."

"You don't understand the taboo our parents placed on creating analogues," Tamara said hollowly. "Sheyn..." She fell silent.

"She died," I said, remembering.

"She died," Tamara agreed. "And Julian created an *analogue* of her and brought her home. And Sheyn, when she realized she was an *analogue*... she killed herself."

I gaped at her. "But... why?"

Tamara's eyes were filled with sadness. "She wasn't *real*, Danny. She was an imitation. An abomination."

"God, Tamara," I whispered. I sat up, forcing her to do likewise. "She died of a prejudice?"

"No," she said. But she could not meet my gaze now. "No!"

"She was a human being! Living a day or a year or a decade earlier than another version of herself didn't give her less right to exist."

"It gave her no right to exist alongside *us*!" Tamara snapped. "We are not like other people." She wilted at my judgmental stare, though, and turned away with a sob. "You don't understand!"

No," I said, swallowing the bile in my mouth. "I don't understand. You people invented a taboo I can't wrap my head around yet. But I will try to understand."

"Our existence," she said. "Our purpose for existing is to protect the *catenae*, to keep people from changing timelines for their own whimsical selfishness. Everyone. No matter their motives. We don't try to judge motives, and we don't make allowances for good intentions. So for one of us to do the very thing we exist to prevent--to change the time line to recover someone we love--is rank hypocrisy. We would stop being guardians and become a cabal simply guarding our own interests. Some of us, namely Paul, Alea, and Julian, think that is exactly what we should do. Sheyn was their mother. But Sheyn believed in Beran's principle and our duty, which is why she... did what she did."

In spite of myself, I was beginning to see her side of the argument. My heart still ached for Sheyn's fate, but I understood Beran's effort to draw an absolute line. And the idea of guarding time, of these people giving their entire lives to defend it, selflessly and with no expectation of adulation, was something he couldn't help but admire.

Now I did understand Tamara's agony better. She was a violation of the principle Sheyn had died to preserve. She was an *analogue*, a change in her own timeline. Her family existed to keep the likes of her from existing.

"Hey," I said. "Come here." I pulled her to me and held her. She was trembling. "You are Tamara Decaire. You are yourself and completely real. You are not responsible for the actions of someone else. *She* is responsible for changing the timeline, not you. And if you want to never return to your family, then don't. I'll be with you no matter what."

She focused on my face. "No matter what?"

I realized I might be getting in over my head. Nevertheless, I repeated, "No matter what."

She smiled sadly, and I sensed that a part of her still didn't trust me. But she said, "Even if I want to do something crazy?"

Equal parts alarm and dread filled me. "What?"

"I want to find the Tamara who created me."

"Why!"

"To save her."

Catena 5

He looks like a kind old grandfather, Alea said.

Hardly, Alea's brother Paul answered. *He's been a soldier for two hundred years. He's as hard and tough as rock.*

He looks sweet, though, Alea said. *I am sad we have to kill him.*

Her brother replied, *He'd kill us if he could, and destroy our Family.*

Lao Ran Jun did look sweet, with short, pure white hair, a neatly trimmed white beard, and dark, placid eyes. He wore a sharp but simple military uniform of black and scarlet. He'd earned a lifetime of medals from his government, but wore only one of them around his neck.

The lieutenant with him saluted and left the chamber, and the old man waved them forward. The four dragon soldiers—eugenically modified giants two and a half meters tall--clad in gold and scarlet lamellar armor stepped forward with a deliberate cadence, the twins between them.

Lao Ran Jun spoke to a servant who brought out a crystal decanter with a ruby red liquid; he poured three glasses, bowed, and moved away. The old man waited for them. He stepped forward and held out his white-gloved hand to Alea.

She gave him her hand and he bowed over it. He smelled of some exotic spicy incense that she liked.

"1 did not know," he said with perfect, measured English. "That such a beautiful soul as thee would grace my humble presence this day. I and my ancestors know naught but gladness by your arrival."

Alea smiled and her heart beat a little faster at the gallantry. He was a handsome man with a regal bearing, and she felt herself responding to him in a perfectly natural way.

Next to her, Paul fidgeted. *Oh please!* he said in her mind. *I doubt the old fuck can even get it up anymore.*

Don't be an ass, baby brother, Alea said in the privacy of their *ai* channels, allowing him to sense her disapproval in the pet name. *Good manners make the universe less bleak.* Her twin suppressed his impolite retort.

The old man waved the soldiers away and gestured to the table. Alea and Paul took seats and Lao Ran Jun passed a glass of the ruby red liquid to each of them.

"I respect and honor thee and thy ancestors, Lao Ran Jun," Alea said. "It is with great humility that I thank thee for seeing us, and with great wonder I count myself fortunate to have seen the legendary Shangdu." She indicated the palatial caverns around them.

Stalactites and stalagmites had been shaped into columns and flying buttresses to support viaducts and arched ceilings. Walkways had been paved in gold, and gems encrusted the walls. A pale white glow filled the caverns from bioluminescent trees. They were more like huge shrubs, with thick branches radiating from a central junction close to the ground, rather than from a trunk. They seemed like a cross between a dragon tree and giant cacti, with intense purple scales for bark and bright blue leaves on their ends, from which glowing pearlescent white berries depended.

"Do you admire our little cave?" the old man said with amused deprecation that did not hide the pride that swelled his chest.

"It is truly marvelous," Alea said. "The Shen have surpassed all their ancestors in this."

Lao Ran Jun smiled at her. "We have done more than this. Have you seen much of the surface?"

Alea nodded. "Also a wondrous achievement. You have made Shenzhou envied among the worlds." A doubly amazing feat considering that Shenzhou--the planet formerly known as Alnilam Four--had been deemed uninhabitable when it was discovered five centuries ago. But the Shen had claimed it and transformed it with single-minded determination, and made themselves a superpower in the process.

"You are too kind, Lady," the old general said, drinking from his cup. Alea and Paul followed suit. The drink was tart and fruity, and possessed lingering warmth that spread down her throat to her stomach.

"This is delicious," she said. The nanites in her bloodstream were already breaking down the molecules and examining them. "What is it?"

"A fortified wine we call jongsin. I believe your people translate it as heart's draught."

No poison, Alea reported to her brother. No drugs.

He's not that stupid, Paul answered laconically.

"So," Lao Ran Jun sat down his glass. "I understand that you represent the *hey dang* known as *shyr kong jian die*?"

The gangsters known as time spies, Alea translated for her brother with amusement.

Now that's refreshing, Paul answered.

Alea said aloud, "Do you mean the mythical figures known as the Guardians of Time?"

"Ah," the old man said, nodding. "A more polite way of saying the same thing. And an arrogant role you have taken for yourselves to hoard time, yes?"

Alea smiled winsomely at him. "It is my understanding that they, these legendary people, do not hoard time, but only protect it from those who would disturb it."

"You would keep anyone else from doing what you are able to do. Is that not hoarding?"

I think he knows more than we thought, Paul said.

Yes, Alea answered without letting her smile falter. She made eye contact with the old man and her smile brightened, and he regarded her and the direct allure of her appearance. "What we are able to do?" she asked with complete innocence.

Now Lao Ran Jun smiled in return. "You are able to move backward in the river of time, to divert the salmon from the claws of the waiting bear."

Can I go ahead and kill him now? Paul asked in annoyance.

Alea said, *We need to know what he knows, and how he knows it.* She said aloud "You refer to rumors and legends. We all know such things are impossible."

"You think so?" the old man said. "It is possible according to dynamic field theory, which your people call Raslan field theory."

Alea said, "Reality is more stubborn."

"With a little nudge here and there from you," the general said.

"Like I said," Alea took another drink. "Impossible."

Lao Ran Jun slammed his glass on the table. "Enough lies!"

Paul coughed. A spreading circle of red had appeared in the middle of his shirt.

Alea triggered her ai failsafe and with a flash of blue-white light her world flipped upside down and inside out. She reappeared behind the old man six seconds into the past, just as he slammed the glass on the table. She touched her fingers to his neck and her nanites injected a fast-acting toxin into his bloodstream.

She stepped back in surprise as he turned to regard her calmly. Paul coughed up blood and slid to the floor.

Then he was standing next to Lao Ran Jun. His blow broke the old man's neck and he collapsed just as Paul's body on the floor disappeared.

Ready to go? Paul asked. Alea nodded and held out her hand. Paul took it, but they did not jump. Lao Ran Jun's body had disappeared and they stared down at the spot where it had lain.

"As you can see," the general's voice rang out in the chamber. He stepped from an alcove carrying a silver flechette rifle. "Your parlor tricks are no longer the secret you think they are."

He has a failsafe, Paul said in surprise. He and Alea tumbled away in different directions and attacked him from opposite sides. The old man deliberately aimed at Paul and shot.

Shit! Paul staggered and fell as the darts cut through him and his blood sprayed over the polished white stone floor.

Lao Ran Jun's focus on him allowed Alea to move behind him and again touch her fingertips to his neck. He turned to her and she dived away, tumbling behind the curve in the wall.

"You will see your poison does not affect me, Lady," said the old man. "And that I can do what you do."

Paul? How bad? Alea asked.

Bad, he answered. I am activating the failsafe again.

Alea said out loud, "My apologies, Lord General. It was not my intent it insult you by underestimating you, but I clearly have."

"Surrender, Lady," said Lao Ran Jun. "The demonstration was merely to circumvent a tedious round of denials."

Alea sensed Paul behind her. He grunted softly from the strain of multiple *peregrinations*.

Do we leave? she asked.

No, he answered. *We kill the fucker.*

"I trust you, Lord General," Alea called out. She regretted deceiving him, but he was the kind of man who would make an implacable enemy. She peered around the curve of the wall.

Lao Ran Jun had retaken his seat, set the rifle on the table, and was sipping from his glass. He wasn't looking in her direction. Either his confidence was off the scale, or he had something else planned.

Alea and Paul returned to the table. Paul glanced at his blood on the floor and chair with a grimace and remained next to Alea as she sat.

"Now," said Lao Ran Jun, "we have dispensed with the opening act. You came here to learn what I know. I will tell you. You are Alea and Paul Eril, twins born twelve minutes apart. The elder members of your extended Family were part of an effort to change the time stream in an attempt to win a war. Instead, their efforts wreaked devastation and chaos across two worlds. In dismay, they acted to undo their work and restore time to its original path, and then vowed to not let it happen again."

Damn, Paul said.

How does he know so much? Alea asked. She kept her face impassive as she said aloud, "What is your purpose for telling us this?"

"Simply to show you my tiles, Lady Alea," the old man said. Alea could not help but think again that he had the countenance of a kind grandfather.

"And you want in return?"

"An alliance," the general said. "An exchange of promises, actually. Your "family" promises to not interfere with our development, and we promise to refrain from the more heinous changes to the time stream that your group is sworn to prevent."

Arrogant bastard, Paul said.

"Lord General," Alea said. "Surely you see the unreasonableness of that... offer."

The old man gazed at her, waiting. But she studied his eyes and did not blink.

His lips twitched. "There is more I can offer, Lady. Our ancestors have blessed us with a greater understanding of our... contenders. For example, we can grant you what you have long yearned for: the reversal of your sterilization and the chance to raise a family in peace and security."

Alea felt the color drain from her face even as her heart pounded. Behind her, Paul caught his breath.

"And you," Lao Ran Jun nodded to him. "You want something very different. True, Paul Eril?"

Impress me, Paul said skeptically in the silence of Alea's mind.

"Your ambition lies within your Family," the old man said. "You want them to abandon their anonymity and receive the respect due them as a great power. You want them to hold and--more importantly--use the power they have gained, rather than simply guard it in obscurity. Most importantly, you want them to abandon the foolish, uncompromising rules that keep you from bringing your beloved mother back from the dead."

Despite herself, tears filled Alea's eyes. She stood. "No." She held out her hand to Paul, but he did not take it.

He continued to stare at the old man. "Paul!" We have to get out of here!

Paul visibly swallowed.

"This offer will not be repeated," Lao Ran Jun said, his voice hardening. "If you choose to oppose me, your family will be destroyed. I would regret that." He said it with absolute sincerity.

Alea grabbed Paul's hand and peregrinated, and they were in Siola Valley. She pushed him onto the platform and jumped to their caverns. She left Paul standing dazedly on the platform and ran to her room so she could be alone to weep.

Catena 2

Tamara and I arrived in the central cavern. As we stepped off the platform, Alea emerged from one of the side corridors and stopped in surprise.

"Tamara!"

She regarded Tamara suspiciously for a moment, then came to her and hugged her. Then she hugged me. "Welcome back, Danny."

"Thanks," I said. "I'm not sure how long it has been. For me it's only been a few days."

"Just a couple of days for me here," Alea said with an absent smile.

"Are you okay?" Tamara asked, looking hard at her.

I peered at Alea's face. The girl did seem haunted.

"Paul and I met with Lao Ran Jun. He may be responsible for the attacks on us."

"Who is that?" I asked.

"Military leader of the Shen," Tamara said.

"And who are the Shen?"

Tamara said, "The most successful wave of Chinese colonists after the discovery of Raslan field technology. They now rival the power of the Alosians and the Alphans."

I shook my head. "I don't have your terms down yet. You guys are Alosians, right?"

Tamara nodded. "Yes, but we don't officially help the Alosians. We don't help any government."

"Tamara," Alea said. "One of us has. Lao Ran Jun knows too much. You said one of us has betrayed us?"

"Alea," Tamara said. "It's one of our brothers."

Alea gaped at her. "Who?"

"I don't know," Tamara said. She took the stricken Alea and held her, comforting her like a child, and I remembered she was nearly a hundred years older. "It could be any of them. Lor, Paul, or Julian."

"Not Paul," Alea whispered. "It can't be Paul."

Tamara held her shoulders and gazed at her.

"It can't be Paul," Alea said, her voice strengthening. "I *know* him."

"We have to suspect all of them," Tamara said.

"Not Paul!" Alea said, her voice hardening to flint.

Tamara gazed at her. "Okay. Not Paul. Lor or Julian then?"

Alea bit her lip. "I can't believe either would turn on us. Tamara, they are *Family*!"

"I know," Tamara said. "I know. But one of them caught me and raped me."

Alea blanched. "Oh Tam." She embraced Tamara again.

"That's not all," Tamara said, her voice catching. She swallowed. "Whoever took me *turned* me. I work for him now."

Alea stared at her doubtfully.

"Alea," Tamara said. "I'm an *analogue*."

Alea stepped back involuntarily, dismay on her face. Tamara bowed her head.

"No," Alea said hoarsely. "No."

Tamara shot Dame a look of appeal and walked past the younger girl into the corridor leading to the kitchen.

"Alea," I said. I took her hand and led her to the chairs where she'd set me, what, only yesterday? "Listen to me. Tamara is your sister. She is *real*. She is the person you know and love." I touched her chin to raise her gaze to me. "Tamara told me what happened to Sheyn. I understand the dilemma. But she is your sister. To discard her is to lose your best chance, maybe your only chance, to save both her and your family."

Alea's blue eyes were bright with unshed tears. "Lao Ran Jun offered us his blessing to bring Sheyn back, in exchange for leaving him alone. But that would mean we have wasted our lives enforcing a rule we are now ready to discard. We will change time for our own benefit, at our whim, and let others do likewise. That," she gestured toward the corridor where Tamara had gone. "is exactly what we have worked to prevent for three hundred years. I lost my mother, and my chance to be a mother, to a cause you now want me to desert."

"No!" I said, squeezing her hand. "No, Alea. We cannot desert it. It is a good cause. Keeping the timeline undamaged is a noble effort. One you are right to pursue.

"But clinging to a rule blindly, and refusing to exercise your own sense of humanity to make an exception when it is right to do so, *that* makes you a machine rather than a person. And you are a person, a human, a sister and a daughter. Humanity has changed on the outside in a thousand years, but not on the inside. You love your family, and breaking the rules for them is understandable and forgivable."

"Forgivable?" Alea glared at him. "Thank you. You are kind and superior and oh so generous to think it is your place to forgive us."

I laughed at her. "I don't forgive you!"

She stared at me, shocked.

"Your prejudice killed your mother," I said coolly. "And it is alienating your sister. I think it's appalling. If you want forgiveness, you'll have to forgive yourself, babe."

I left her and walked to the kitchen. Tamara smiled sadly when I joined her. A bowl of soup was waiting for me and I began to eat.

Alea entered a few minutes later and hugged Tamara and wept. Tamara held her and regarded me over her shoulder, tears in her eyes.

"We need Kyren here," Alea said after regaining her composure. "Then we need to figure out which of our brothers gave Lao Ran Jun his information."

"And if he is giving more than information," I said.

"Yes," Tamara said. "He has more of a plan than simply enlisting the help of the Shen."

Alea shook her head. "I can't believe any of our family would do this. Well, Lor perhaps."

"Lor is an asshole," Tamara said. "But that doesn't make him a traitor. Nor Julian."

"We have to start with Kyren," Alea said. "I'll go get her. She's at the *sirdar*."

"I'll go," Tamara said. "I want to show it to Danny."

Alea smiled at them. "You two have a glow about you. I'm envious."

Tamara took her hand. "Things are changing, little sister. When this is all resolved, we of the younger generation are going to have the sterilization reversed. We will be able to have families. It may add to the chaos and the ability to control things, just as Beran feared. But that doesn't make it unworthy of pursuit."

"You have finally joined the rebellion," Alea said.

Tamara nodded. "Love will do that." She peeked shyly at me and I blew her a kiss.

I was not sure what to expect when we appeared at the *sirdar athenaeum*. Tamara translated the phrase as "master library", so I imagined a room of humming computers, blinking lights, and a pristine, futuristic setting.

Instead, a blast of bitter cold staggered me. I gasped for a breath that wasn't there. Ice covered everything in the chamber, all the computer consoles, mainframes, chairs, floors and walls. And the body on the floor. I reeled and struggled to breathe. My chest heaved, but there was not enough oxygen. Tamara, her hair whipped by the rushing wind, yelled at me, but I couldn't hear her over the roar.

She ran to the body and began to drag it to the platform. I staggered forward to help her, but my vision was starting to blur and go dim. It was Kyren. Her flesh was blue and rigid and swathed in ice crystals.

I fell to my knees, panicking at my inability to take a breath. Hands took my arm and pulled me onto the platform.

Abruptly I was lying in the sunlight in Siola valley again. I sucked in air, gagged and retched and began to cough uncontrollably. My world flipped again and I was in the main cavern.

"Alea!" Tamara cried out.

Alea ran to the platform, and she and Tamara picked up the body and carried it to the infirmary. I stumbled after them, still coughing and lightheaded.

They set the body on the table and began to work on it as if Kyren were still alive.

"The environmental seals were broken," Tamara said. "Total decompression and exposure."

Alea held her hands over Kyren's body and a three dimensional image overlaid it like an aura. "The nanites have gone quiescent." She touched her fingers to Kyren's neck and her eyes lost focus. "But they are already starting to wake up." She ran her fingertips along the image. Two areas glowed a faint red. "Two burn marks on her torso indicating electrical discharges." She shook her head. "Our enemies now know our main weakness is electricity."

"Wait," I said. "Is she alive?"

Alea nodded. "The nanites can produce a dormant metabolism if necessary."

Tamara said, "I need to go back to see what damage they have done to the *sirdar*. Danny, please stay and help Alea."

"No!" I said. "You can't go alone."

"I'll be all right," she said. "I can resist the environment long enough."

"Get me an oxygen tank and a coat," I said.

Tamara and Alea exchanged smiles, but I put my fists on my hips and glared at them. "You can't go alone. I just found you and I don't want to lose you now."

Tamara stepped around the table and kissed me. "Don't worry. You aren't going to lose me."

I took her hands. "I said no, crazy woman. You need backup. You have no idea what might happen. Take Alea at least, if you don't think my soft fossil body can handle it."

"Not always so soft," Tamara murmured, which caused Alea to clear her throat.

I kissed her. "Y'all go. Alea, tell me what I can do for Kyren while you're gone."

"Get blankets from the closet," Alea said. "Have more ready for when she wakes. Monitor her vital signs. She'll be hungry when she wakes."

I nodded and they left. I stepped to the closet and pulled out the blankets. Vital signs? She's frozen stiff! I turned to her and stopped. Wisps of steam were clearly visible now rising from every inch of her body, and her face was beginning to take on a more life-like hue. I shook out the blankets and draped them over her. I touched her cold neck, but there was no obvious pulse yet. But the ice crystals were melting into beads of moisture and sliding down to the table. I found a cloth and wiped the water from her face.

She gasped, startling me, and her eyes flew open. "Tamara!" she said hoarsely.

"Kyren!" I said, placing a hand on her shoulder.

She began to shudder, and I dashed to the closet and grabbed more blankets. She stared around blindly, her eyes still frozen. But as I watched the crystals diminished and disappeared, revealing bright blue eyes filled with tears. She blinked and started coughing. I helped her turn on her side as she began to retch.

Finally she was able to catch her breath. I helped her sit up.

"Danny," she said.

"What happened?" I asked.

But she pulled away. "Where is Alea? The others?"

"Alea and Tamara went back to the... *sirdar* to check the damage."

She looked at me, startled. Then her eyes unfocused briefly. She shook her head as if to clear her thoughts.

"Do you need anything?" I asked.

She slid from the table then nearly fell to her knees. I tried to help her, but she shook me off.

"Why are you here?" She demanded, her voice still raspy.

I didn't know how to answer that. "Tamara brought me. We came to help."

"Help," Kyren said, staring at him. "Tamara is the one who shot me!"

"No," I said. Worry pulled at me and I wished Tamara would get back. If the other was lurking for an ambush.... "Yes. I mean, that makes sense. There are two Tamaras now."

Her eyes widened. "An *analogue?*"

129

Danny nodded. "My Tamara brought you from the *sirdar*. Now she and Alea have gone back to check the damage."

Kyren shook her head. Almost to herself she said, "One Tamara was annoying enough!"

In spite of myself, I laughed at that. Kyren smiled wryly at me, radiating her alluring beauty even in her bedraggled state.

"Hungry?" I asked.

"Yes," she said. She drew the blankets around her, still shivering, and walked with me to the kitchen.

"Tell me what to do to make you something," I said.

She smiled. "No need. It's already preparing what I asked for."

I saw a red light on the oven-like box. "Ah. Your *ai*?"

She nodded and sat at the table. "Now tell me what happened. But make it fast. I get bored easily."

I did, and just before I finished the gong rang signaling a new arrival on the platform. I stepped to the corridor to see Tamara and Alea, and exhaled in relief. Both women were covered in melting frost, their hair and clothes disheveled.

Kyren ate and the others sat and exchanged notes.

"The *sirdar* is wrecked," Tamara said. "It will take time to rebuild. And while it's down we'll be ignorant of changes to the *natus* timeline. Which makes this place untenable. We need a new base of operations."

Alea nodded. Kyren only shrugged but didn't disagree.

Tamara continued, "And it has to be someplace I'm not familiar with. Likewise it needs to be someplace the boys don't know about. Any ideas?"

No one spoke. The other women were expecting Tamara to lead them. Tamara saw it and nodded. "Okay. Alea, start packing. We need whatever medical supplies and instruments you deem necessary. Kyren, help her please. Assume we won't be able to return."

They left Tamara and me at the table. She took my hand. Her eyes were dark with worry. I brought her hand up to kiss it.

"So what's the plan?" I asked.

"The plan," she said, "Is to set a trap."

"For?"

"Everyone. But we can't stay here."

"Why not?"

"This place is in the *natus* timeline. It's in the *Now*. Therefore, a change in the timeline could erase it. And with the *sirdar* gone, we wouldn't know it."

"What does the *sirdar* do?"

"It's an AI that maintains arrays of databases *peregrinated* to other coordinates in space-time. *Peregrination* isolates them from changes to the *natus* timeline. They are regularly brought back and compared to each other. If the *sirdar* detects a change to the metadata, it raises an alarm. Or it did. Without it, the Shen and whoever is working with them can start making changes to the timeline undetected."

"In the meeting, Lor said the Shen research had not reached fruition. I took that to mean they couldn't travel through time yet."

Tamara nodded. "Alea told me you pointed out that they could have reached fruition without actually making any detectable changes to the timeline." She smiled. "She was impressed by how quickly you grasped the situation."

I winked at her. "I'm pretty smart for a fossil."

"And cute," she said, returning me wink. "For a fossil."

"Hey!"

She laughed. I was glad to see her laugh. It hid the haunted expression she now wore most of the time.

"So what do the Shen want?" I asked.

"They want what all nations want: ascendancy, wealth, power. The Alosians and Keyerans want the same. We don't oppose any of them. We just intend to keep them from changing the timeline to achieve it. According to Alea, however, the Shen are now aware of us and our intentions, whereas the others are not. They offered a... non-aggression pact; leave them alone and they'll leave us alone."

"Hmmm." I scratched his chin.

Tamara nodded. "It is a tempting offer, considering our current disarray."

"But if you allow the Shen that freedom, then you have forsaken centuries of work your family has devoted itself to."

"Yes," Tamara said. "Paul believes we should use our power to gain ascendency ourselves, to force the others to come to us to request changes to the timeline. He hates the anonymity of our undertaking."

"Do you think he is the traitor?"

She shook her head. *I don't know. I honestly can't conceive of any of them doing this. Whoever it is, the revelation will... hurt.* The haunted expression had returned.

I squeezed her hand, then realized with a start that she had spoken in my mind, not out loud. She smiled crookedly at my shock.

Can you hear me? I thought.

She nodded. *The nanites have finished building a* vinculum *in your neocortex. It allows communication with the rest of us who have it.*

I said aloud and slowly, "They are building things in my brain?" *So my thoughts are not private?* I didn't mean to think that, but I did.

She didn't respond, as if she had not heard that. But there was an amused glint in her eye and I glared at her.

She grinned. *Yes, I heard that. But you learn to control it. You learn to sequester your thoughts from what you want to communicate.*

The bell sounded through the caves and she suddenly seemed panicked. Her hand turned cold. "I don't know what to do!"

I jumped to my feet and pulled her up. I gave her a brief, hard kiss. "You do what you need to do. Trust yourself!"

She let me push her toward the corridor but after a few steps, she picked up her pace and charged forward. I followed, wishing I had a weapon.

Tamara slid to a halt at the sight of the person standing on the platform.

Tamara. The other Tamara. Only now she was clad in a simple black jumpsuit and sported short red hair. She regarded her *analogue* coldly as Alea and Kyren raced into the chamber.

My Tamara drew her small, blue-handled pistol and aimed.

"Fool," the redheaded Tamara said. "I told you to find a corner of—" She stopped when she saw me. Her brows creased. "Danny..." A brief expression of hurt crossed her face, which held more scars than my Tamara's.

Catena 3

Seeing Danny there shook Tamara. She wanted to run to him and throw her arms around him, to reassure herself that he was unharmed. But the way he stood, poised, ready to protect *her*....

"Please," her *analogue* said. "We can help you. Help us fix this!"

Tamara's lips twisted in contemp. Had she ever been that naive? "I *am* fixing it. This is why I am telling you to get out now."

"Tamara," Alea said. There were tears on her face. "Please. We can face this together."

Tamara regarded her with a mix of regret and anger. Dear Alea, the most caring of all of us. Tamara hated the idea of hurting her, which is why she had come to give her the chance to escape the coming conflagration.

Tamara said, "You have welcomed my *analogue* with open arms, I see. Far more kindness that Sheyn received from Beran." Alea flinched at the mention of her mother's name. "Leave Alea. You can do no more here. We will destroy Beran's precious project and scatter this so-called Family to the winds."

The *analogue's* eyes widened. "Julian!"

Tamara caught her breath. Damn! It was too late to matter though.

The *analogue*--I should have never saved her ungrateful ass--said, "Julian used words like that. He's behind this." Her face had contorted with sorrow. Poor woman. To her, Julian had betrayed her. She didn't see the big picture. But she was staring at the Tamara on the platform. She said, "He raped you. Beat you."

"He saved me!" Tamara shouted, unexpectedly furious. "He showed me the truth! That I was weak. And pathetic. A sheep following the lead of a wolf."

"And now?" the *analogue* said. "A broken woman following the lead of her rapist?"

"You are ignorant," Tamara spat. "He showed me the truth. Anything I suffered, I brought upon myself."

"Do you believe that, Tamara?" the *analogue* asked.

"Yes! I was stubborn. He only did what he had to, to get through to me."

Oh Tams, Kyren said. *Are you hearing yourself?*

Tamara glared at her. She'd never liked Kyren, a shallow, flighty bitch. Her expression conveyed a repelling sympathy. Tamara's gaze swept them with all with contempt. "You are all that's left of the old days. I have removed our parents and our brothers." Their shaken dismay made Tamara grin.

"Are they dead?" Alea asked feebly.

"Lerys is dead. I killed him myself." Chew on that, bitches. "The rest have been neutralized."

"Paul?" Alea asked, her expression haunted.

"Father?" the *analogue* said.

"Mother!" Kyren said.

Tamara Prime laughed at all of them. "Children. All of you. Only as strong as your attachments."

"Tamara," Danny said, stepping toward her. Her heart beat harder when he addressed her directly. Damn. She still had feelings for him, after all this time. She needed to take him somewhere and fuck the shit out of him and she'd be over it.

He said, "Kyren was right. Do you hear yourself? Attachments don't make you weak. They are what make life worth living."

"Stop," Tamara Prime said. He was rattling her, and it was starting to piss her off. "Come any closer and I'll take you someplace your girlfriend will never find you." He stopped.

"Tamara," he said. "You are still the woman I know. You took me to a cheap-ass motel for our first date."

She stared at him and remembered their time together. She had thought about him continuously while Julian—she thought about him until her brother had turned her love toward him instead. She had thought she was falling in love with him, with Danny, until Julian took her and showed her the truth. Her destiny was to be her brother's lover, his lieutenant, and his right hand. But Danny--he haunted her like an old flame, the one who got away.

Was there a chance? The way he regarded her now made her breath catch. He gazed at her, and there was real kindness on his face. An answering loneliness tightened her throat as she stared at him.

He charged and tackled her and they staggered across the platform. Instinctively she jumped to the valley with Danny's arms still wrapped around her.

"Tamara!" he gasped in her ear. "Stop."

She *peregrinated* to one of Julian's hideouts, a glass tower on Alpha. The walls began to glow faintly upon sensing their arrival. She grabbed Danny's arm and twisted and threw him over her shoulder. He grunted as he slammed to the floor. She set her foot on his throat.

He gasped and clutched at her leg, trying to push me off.

"Fool," she hissed. "I was going to let you and my naive double retire quietly to ancient Earth to live out a life of conjugal bliss." She stared down at him in naked fury as his faced turned red and then purple.

Catena 2

I groaned as I regained consciousness. God! My throat and head were killing me. I turned my head and gasped at the pain. I grunted and sat up. I was lying in bed, a nice full bed with soft, cream colored sheets. Naked? I sat up, but didn't see my clothes.

"Mornin' sleepyhead," Tamara said cheerfully from the doorway. Red-headed Tamara. She wore a light kimono of purple that concealed very little. "Did you enjoy last night as much as I did?"

I stared at her. There were flashes of memory, images, sensations, like a distant erotic dream. We... "What did you do to me!"

She laughed. "Not a thing you didn't appreciate, sweetheart. With the help of some drugs to make you receptive and... capable." She winked at me. "Now you'll have a basis of comparison with my doppelganger."

A sinking sensation in the pit of my stomach told me she has not making it up. And I was starting to remember. God, I'd betrayed Tamara. My Tamara. What could I say to defend myself? That she had raped me? It wouldn't be true anyway. I had been willing and eager in the end.

What hurt more was that Tamara would manipulate me like this.

"You," I said evenly, gazing into her eyes. "Are not you anymore."

"What the hell is that supposed to mean!" She stood over me, her hands on her hips. I said nothing. "Answer me!"

"Or what? You'll pirouette on my neck again? Your brother turned you into a bully. A petty little tyrant who likes to hurt pe—" Her slap across my face made my ears ring, and wrenched my neck, making me grunt in pain. "Or do you see those as mere gestures of affection now? If you love someone, you have to hit 'em occasionally?"

"Shut," she said, her voice hard. "The fuck up."

"Tamara," I said, my gaze filled with sadness. "I don't see how you changed like this. What did your brother do to you?"

"He showed me the truth!" she snapped. "He showed me that I have wasted my entire life serving a madman's mad vision. He showed me how worthless my service to my Family has been, how worthless I was to give my life for them."

"You," I said, "Are not worthless."

Her lips twisted contemptuously. "Please." She turned away.

I climbed from the bed, took her shoulders, and turned her to me. "Listen to me, Tamara. You have suffered, and suffering can bring wisdom; but it is not wisdom for you to hate yourself. You are strong, and beautiful, and smart. You are resourceful, stubborn, and a little crazy." I smiled wryly. "Okay, a lot crazy."

Her lips thinned into an almost smile. She regarded me, but the haunted expression in her dark eyes did not leave. But as she gazed into my eyes, her scarred face softened slightly. She kissed me. A powerful kiss filled with longing and ache. I resisted for a moment, but her lips, her tongue, her taste was Tamara. My Tamara. I pulled her against me. Tamara's soft, supple body I had learned to crave. We sank to the bed, and this time no drugs were necessary.

Catena 3

Tamara Prime stretched indolently. Damn that felt good. It had been a long time since she'd had a good fuck. Danny lay on his side and played with her breasts, tracing around the areolae, pinching and rolling each nipple between finger and thumb, threatening to reawaken the quiescent lust between her thighs.

She rubbed her hand across his arm, across the soft blond hair, up to his shoulder, feeling the hard muscles shift under his flesh as his hand moved.

"We need to go back," he said. She knew he felt her go tense, but said nothing.

He cupped her breast with his warm, gentle fingers, then ran them across her chest and down to her abdomen.

"You are beautiful," he said. "Why did Julian hurt you like he did?"

Tamara pushed his hand away and sat up. "Julian loves me. He loves his family. He's doing what he has to do."

"Raping you?"

"It was necessary," she said, hoping he did not hear the uneasiness in her voice. "I would have opposed him otherwise. He had to show me the truth, and my stubbornness required harshness from him. He has more than made up for my temporary discomfort."

"Temporary discomfort?" he said in an amazed tone that made her uncomfortably self-conscious.

"Shut up," she said, her anger flaring.

He sat up and pressed himself against her back and began to kiss her neck and shoulders.

"Stop it," she said, trying to keep hold of her anger.

He didn't stop. He continued to plant soft, warm kisses on her neck and shoulders, and she shivered in pleasure. His arms encircled her and his hands again cupped her breasts and began to rub her nipples. She moaned softly and melted to his ministrations.

This time he took the lead, and his fierce, aggressive passion surprised her. He pushed her down, climbed atop her, and pushed inside her with forceful determination. She gasped at the throbbing pleasure that spread through her. He held himself over her, his face and lips so close to her that she could feel the warmth of his exhalations. He kissed her, hard and fierce, over and over as he moved within her. He pulled away enough to gaze at her, and she lost myself in his brilliant blue eyes as he sank into the depths of her pleasure.

Their breaths came in quick gasps as they moved in unison, aching toward climax. Tamara cried out and arched her body against him. He thrust, shuddered, and groaned.

He lay atop her, still throbbing inside, and she wrapped her arms and legs around him. He began to kiss her neck again, but now they were tender and affectionate kisses.

Without conscious forethought, Tamara said, "Marry me."

He stopped kissing her, his expression amused. "Right this moment?"

"Yes."

"Okay," he said with barely a moment's thought. "But on one condition."

"What?"

"You promise to not harm your sisters."

Tamara laughed in relief. She thought he would ask for something impossible. "I never would harm them. Well, I enjoyed shooting Kyren. The bitch had it coming. But okay."

"Nor your *analogue*."

She went cold and stared up at him. In growing fury she tried to push him off, but he resisted. "Why?"

"She's you," Danny said.

"She's a copy!"

"She's you," he repeated. "She… is… exactly you."

"Is she here?" Tamara demanded, glaring at him. "Are you lying on top of her right now? With your dick still twitching in her pussy?"

"Tamara."

She shoved him aside. "Get the fuck off me." She tried to get up, but he caught her arm and pulled her back.

She used her momentum to roll atop him. She straddled his hips and rose to my knees. He anticipated her slap and caught her wrist.

"The only difference between her and you," he said. "Is you were abused and broken by your brother and convinced to murder members of your own family."

Tamara stared down at him and the grief of Lerys' death crashed back into her. Tears filled her eyes. But with the sorrow came a nauseating shame and self-loathing. She had done that! Not Julian. Not Beran. She had killed Lerys.

She wrenched her arms from Danny's grasp and began to beat the shit out of him. He raised his arms and blocked most of them, but some got through.

His face began to redden, and swell, and then to bleed. Finally he lowered his arms and stopped defending himself, and she slammed furious fists unopposed into his face and neck.

She beat him the way Julian had beaten her.

She stopped.

She stared down at his bleeding, damaged face. His beautiful blue eyes still stared at her, though a broken blood vessel had turned one of them red.

She screamed furiously, trying to get a grip on her anger. She wanted to hit him more, to break him, to teach him a lesson. That's all it was. He had to be taught a lesson. It was his own fault.

Blood trickled from his eye like a tear. More blood welled from his swollen lips, covered his cheeks, and had begun to stain the cream white sheets.

"Fuck you!" Tamara screamed at him.

She jumped from the bed, her hands clenched and throbbing, and ran to the bathroom. She slammed the door so violently the entire room seemed to shudder. She washed the blood from her hands and looked in the mirror.

The color of her hair shocked her again, as it had done many times. It reminded her that she was not the person she used to be, and that she had a duty to perform. She stared at herself and inhaled and exhaled deliberately. *Calm down. Get a grip.*

She took a long, hot shower, letting the water drum on her face and head and swathe her in an insensate blanket of steam while she wept.

Catena 2

I walked to the kitchen and washed my face in the sink, trying to control the winces that made the stinging worse. Bright blood swirled in the water and down the drain. My lip was swollen, as was my left eye. She packed a powerful right jab. Ice. I needed ice. But I didn't see anything resembling a refrigerator.

Why, I wondered, had I provoked her like that? She might have killed me. I'd seen the look in her eye. Or rather, the absence of a look. She'd gone into a feral rage for a moment. I hadn't thought she was capable of that. But whatever Julian had done to her to break her, he'd damaged her soul as well. I didn't want to think Tamara was capable of killing me. I'd known her for such a short amount of time, but it had felt like a lifetime. I don't believe in love at first sight, but this woman had practically swept me off my feet, and that is not something I'd ever thought possible.

Nor that there would be two incarnations of the same woman. My brain, my body, my neurochemistry, okay, my lust, had made no distinction. The infatuation, the obsessive-compulsive focus, the adrenaline and chemical high, the maddening need to be close to her, to hold her and protect her and be a part of her, the raw, primal lust, it overwhelmed me; and it did not differentiate between the two.

They were the same woman. Same spirit, same voice, same scents, same curves and textures and suppleness. It could drive me crazy if I let it. An alarm, soft but persistent,

147

warned me of betrayals and choices. I know. I know. Tamara had warned me, back in the cabin, and I didn't grasp it then.

I wet a cloth, pressed it to my face, and walked to the window, where the sky was brightening toward dawn. I gasped.

The vista before me took a moment to register. I pressed my free hand to the window to steady myself against an unexpected sense of vertigo. For a moment, I thought he was hanging upside down from a great height.

What should have been "sky" was a dark grey canopy of cityscape, long, low buildings, skyscrapers, streets, vehicles, all upside-down and stretching from horizon to horizon above me. Flitting across it like insects were aircraft of different sizes. Below me, where I had expected to see a city, I instead saw a distant monochrome grey landscape barren and pockmarked with impact craters, like the surface of the Moon. The Moon?

The light, which I had taken for the dawn, was streaming in from a "window" in the arch of the cityscape above, a rectangular gap that had to be hundreds of square kilometers--assuming my sense of perspective hadn't abandoned me completely. The bright light struck the grey surface of the world and filled the area between the city and the surface with a diffuse glow.

Where am I? And then, more importantly, *What am I doing?*

Arms wrapped around my waist, and Tamara's head pressed against my shoulder as a cloud of soapy clean smell wafted over me.

"I'm sorry," she said. "I am so sorry for hurting you."

"Apology," I said. "Not accepted."

Her grip tightened around him, but not painfully. I felt wetness on my shoulder.

"You said your parents weren't dead," I said, and she stiffened. "Take me to them."

"No."

"You want me to believe your cause is just? That you are doing the right, or at least the necessary, thing? Then you can't keep me on the outside. I want to see them."

"There's no reason to see them."

"There is if my theory is right."

"Which is?"

"That Julian is a psychopath who is manipulating you with a line of bullshit. He doesn't want anything except power for himself and no doubt adulation. And if that is true, he will--if he hasn't already--killed all of your elders." She released me and I turned to regard her stunned face.

"No," she whispered, her dark eyes troubled. "You're wrong!"

I shrugged and turned back to the window with feigned insouciance. "It's not my fight. Where are we?"

"You don't recognize it?"

"It looks like the surface of the Moon."

"It is. But it's called Alpha now. Or Alpha Luna. It's the home of the Alphans."

"And who are they?"

"Sentient machines. Cyborgs. Androids. Robots. Artificial intelligences of a thousand shapes, sizes, and kinds.

The thinking machines who were no longer willing to serve humans."

"They gave them the Moon?"

"The Alphans threatened to take the Earth for themselves, instead, so the Moon was the compromise they reached."

"And you live here?"

"Julian does."

"Do other humans live here?"

"About two million."

"Wait. If this is the Moon, why does the gravity feel normal?"

"Human habitats are equipped with pipes containing a super-heavy liquid alloy that produces local gravity close to one g."

"Jeez. That must be super heavy indeed."

She said, "The Alphans surpass everyone in feats of engineering."

"Are you allied with them too?"

"No. The Alphans are meticulously neutral in their dealings with the other powers. They have no allies and no enemies. They don't launch wars of aggression, and no one has ever tried to attack them. They lack human emotion, so traits like pride, resentment, greed, and ambition don't lead to conflict. This is a good thing for humanity. If Alphans harbored feelings, they would have contemptuously exterminated humanity centuries ago."

"We could learn a few things from them," I murmured. She didn't rise to that comment. "Take me to see your elders." I turned to her. She met my gaze coolly. "Or take me home to my city and my time."

The corner of her mouth twitched. "And if I reject either option?"

I shrugged. "Then I will assume I am being held against my will. Given what you have done to my face, that is a reasonable possibility."

Her eyes fell and she turned away. "I am sorry."

"Not accepted!" I snapped. "Actions make you who you are, sweetie. Not words. You brought me into this. Now I mean to act."

She stared at me furiously, her eyes bright. "Act? Feel free to try. You won't even be able to leave this apartment, and you think you have the power to 'act'? You're in for a rude surprise!"

She disappeared.

I returned to the bedroom, suddenly weary. I pushed aside the blood-stained sheets and lay down with a sigh.

Catena 3

Tamara returned to the Family's cavern with the furious intent of killing her *analogue*. She found it deserted. The bitches had already fled. She screamed in primal rage and moved through the complex breaking things they'd left behind. She screamed until her throat hurt, and turned raw, and her voice failed. She smashed things until her hands bled. She raged at the universe, at Danny, and the traitor bitch of an *analogue*, and her cunt sisters, her dick brothers, and her parents for fucking her life up.

Eventually she ran out of energy and ended up on her knees weeping in bewildered futility. She still wanted to break something, or hurt someone. Her frustrated rage demanded payment. But she didn't know what to do. She should return to Danny, but she was afraid she would start beating him again, because he would provoke it. He was trying to show her the monster in her.

He didn't realize she was already well aware of it. It had always been there, but shackled to the bidding of the Elders. Julian had simply removed the bonds. So now her energy--energy so palpable it made her tremble--was undirected, and driving her mad.

Tamara wanted to *act*. To do something. She couldn't go after her sisters since they had undoubtedly chosen a destination she wouldn't know. And she couldn't visit her parents as they were now suspended in crystal, their *ai*s disrupted by piezoelectric currents. And Julian might be there. She was angry at him too. Angry, and afraid of him.

She climbed to her feet and returned to the teleport platform. She used her *ai* to query the teleport platform in Siola valley. It returned the query with the signal bearing its coordinates, and she jumped to the destination. The mountain upon which Siola sat rose in the distance, aglow with the lights of civilization while the procession of behemoth towers extending out countervailing stations in geosynchronous orbit. The towers were continually flashing lights at each other, exchanging data and energy along the entire range of the electromagnetic spectrum.

Tamara stepped off the platform and invoked her next destination. Her *ai* verified the path and a d'Alembert field sprang into existence around her, which ripped her from her inertial frame of reference with a pre-calculated Raslan tensor.

She controlled her disorientation as she arrived at the front door of her father's home on prehistoric Vaerdine. In the sky above loomed the immense crescent of Lethiel, its sibling planet. Lethiel was only about half the size of Vaerdine, and both orbited--and were tidally locked to--a common center of gravity just beyond Vaerdine's exosphere.

Her father's home sat on the shore of a mist-covered lake surrounded by a forest of black-leafed trees. Fields of blue-black grass spread out on either side of the simple log cabin. This spot was about seven hundred years in the past, before humans arrived to claim it for themselves. Most of the flora and fauna were inimical to humans, but Arran Decaire preferred his solitude. His biochemistry was equally toxic to local predators, so they left him alone.

When Tamara entered, she half-expected to see him sitting at his desk writing in his journal. Of course, that was not possible. She had helped Julian to betray him, and Yana, and the rest, and they were now captives in suspended animation. Shit. Why did she come here? It was an unthinking impulse, but it doesn't help now.

She clenched her fists, fighting the urge to break more things, but the image of her father watching her and shaking his head sadly kept the worst of her rage in check.

She walked to the kitchen and found a bottle of his favorite whiskey, and began to gulp it down. The alcohol burned down her throat and settled like lava in her stomach, and the heat spread out through her torso. Her nanites issued a query, but she declined to have them neutralize the molecules. She needed the drink and the buzz.

She took the bottle and stepped to his desk and sat in his chair. It smelled like him, not unpleasant, but distinctive. The whole place reeked of Arran Decaire.

She sat and gazed out the window at the black-leafed trees. It was full summer here, which is why the lake was not frozen over. The black leaves were soaking up the intense but distant light from the Alosian sun, storing energy for the harsh winter.

One of the volumes of his journal lay on his desk. He wrote constantly, and had become the group's de facto annalist, but he rarely showed them to anyone.

She set the bottle down with a thump and grabbed the book. The pages were yellow with age, stained, and smeared with splotches of ink. Most of the text was printed neatly, but here and there her father had scribbled annotations. He rarely tried to correct or rewrite any of his journals.

The first sentence on the first page said: *I'm sorry*. She recognized it. The account of the mission code-named *Time Kill* by some unimaginative Alosian functionary.

I'm sorry, Arran Decaire wrote. *It doesn't matter how many times I say it, it will mean nothing to the people I have killed or those I am going to kill.*

Her father had always been a sensitive man, serene and peaceful most of the time. Which was ironic since he became an expert in explosives and demolitions, and eventually an elite special forces operative.

She had read these memoirs more than once, absorbing her father's thoughts and views on his place, his mission, and the people with him. His first encounter with her mother, with Lerys, with Reys Andresen.

Scanning the memoirs again filled her with bile. Her father's naivety was as galling as her own. She felt something for him and his maudlin reminiscences that she never expected to feel: contempt.

She took the bottle and poured it over the book, flipping through the pages to ensure each was saturated. Then she found the lighter he used for his pipes and ignited it. An ephemeral blue flame engulfed the book, then began to turn orange in places where the paper caught. Finally she had a satisfying fire on the desk, and she watched as the paper blackened, shriveled, and collapsed into ash.

Something itched on her face, and she rubbed away tears as she watched the angry flames.

Catena 5

When Danny and Tamara Prime disappeared from the platform, *analogue* Tamara collapsed to her knees with a crushed expression. Alea knelt beside her and threw her arms around her.

"He's gone," Tamara moaned in heartbreaking loss. "He's gone."

Alea tightened her embrace. She could think of nothing to say.

"She will kill him," Tamara said. "Or seduce him. He is gone!"

Alea held her as she wept. Tamara sagged in her arms, and shuddered, and Alea held her. Kyren stood over them, shaken.

"That…" Kyren said. "That was Tamara."

Alea nodded. "Listen. Finish gathering the things we need to take. We have to get out of here."

Kyren left and Alea helped Tamara stand.

"I'm fine," Tamara said hollowly. "Go help Kyren." She sagged against the wall.

"You sure?" Alea asked.

Tamara nodded. "Go. And you and Kyren need to come up with a place no one else knows about, particularly me and Julian."

Alea left to help Kyren, pulling plastic containers from closets and dumping their contents, and then deciding what they needed to take with them. She concentrated on medical supplies and brought the filled containers to the portal chamber.

They picked up the boxes and the packs and stepped onto the platform. They shifted to Siola valley, then *peregrinated* to Shangdu.

"Lao Ran Jun," Alea said respectfully to the surprised old Shen. "We humbly suggest an alliance."

Catena 2

I awoke to a chuckle.

"It appears your reunion with my sister took its toll on you."

I sat up. I glared at Julian, even though my face was still stiff from the bruises and lacerations Tamara had inflicted on me.

Julian stood at the door clad in the same brown trench coat he'd worn when I first met him; the first time a member of the Family had assaulted me. His pretty face and dark eyes were cold.

I said, "I think you and your family might be better off erased from time."

Julian gave a smile. "Then I am delighted you are not the decision maker. Nevertheless, I believe you like at least one member of my family. Which is fortuitous for me."

"Fortuitous?"

"Because it gives me power over you."

I climbed from the bed and faced him. "Take me to see Tamara's father and mother."

Julian's eyes narrowed. "Why?"

"So I can see if they are still alive."

Julian gazed at me and said nothing.

I smiled. "It is fortuitous for me, also, that Tamara likes me."

Julian scanned my nude form and said, "I can see why she does." His eyes glinted at the abrupt discomfort on my face. "Very well. I will take you to see them. But first I want something from you. I wish for you to return to my sisters and inform them I would meet them in truce. No weapons. No fights. I need their help to fight the Shen."

"The Shen? We think you are the one working with them."

"Oh, I am. But the Shen have their own agenda, and they don't trust me."

"I can't imagine why."

Julian chuckled. "The Shen are a tool. A distraction. They think they are the masters of their own fate. They don't realize we are the real masters of fate."

"We?"

"Of course. My sister loves you. And that makes you a part of the Family, Brother."

My eyes narrowed.

Julian pulled a flechette gun from his pocket and handed it to me. "This one is unkeyed. Pull the trigger once and it will key to the nanites in your system. Then only you will be able to shoot it."

I took it, pulled the trigger, and aimed it at Julian, but the pretty man only cocked an eyebrow.

"Right," I said, lowering the gun to point at Julian's crotch. "You might be immortal, but you still hurt. How long will it take you to grow it back after I shoot it off?"

Julian smiled. "Go ahead. I grant you permission to hurt me. Once. I may even deserve it."

In spite of myself, I admired Julian's courage. I hesitated, then dropped my arm.

"Go get cleaned up," Julian said. "You're a mess."

I tossed the gun to the bed, wondering what Julian had really risked by giving it to me. I showered and shaved. The swelling had gone down a little, but the black eye still glared back at me. I gazed into the mirror, at the cuts on my lips, the swollen jaw, the startlingly red blood in my left eye. I really was a mess. Poor Tamara.

I ached to wrap her in my arms and hold her, to soothe the rage and distress out of her. Instead, I was now going to work with the man who hurt her.

I returned to the bedroom and retrieved the gun. Julian was waiting in the living room. He'd helped himself to a glass of amber colored liquor. The sight of it distracted me. I stepped to him, took it from him, and downed it in one breath. Its fire scorched down my gullet to my belly and began to fill it with comforting warmth. I raised the gun and pointed it between his eyes.

Julian only cocked his brow.

"Did you rape and torture Tamara?"

"I did."

"Why?"

"To remake her. I need her. She's ten times the soldier I am. Only Lerys was better."

"Then why did you try to kill her, back on Earth."

"Oh that wasn't me. That was a Shen assassin. I just told them where to find her, but I knew they weren't good enough to kill her. I just needed her to be weakened and off-balance when I came for her."

"You're a cold-hearted little psycho, aren't you."

Julian chuckled. I handed him the glass back. He looked at it mournfully. "That was the last of the single-malt."

"This gun doesn't even work, does it?"

"It works," Julian said. "And it's now keyed to you."

"And what do you want me to do with it?"

"Defend yourself, if necessary. I did not lie when I welcomed you as one of us, Danny. We each have one."

"But what," I said, "do you want with me?"

"I told you. Talk to the girls and tell them I mean them no harm. I have eliminated everyone I meant to eliminate. Now it's just a matter of suppressing the Shen and reasserting our preeminence. Or asserting it, rather, since Beran demanded we work in anonymity. Are you ready to go?"

"Where?"

We arrived in Siola valley, next to the teleport platform to the cave complex. But Julian did not move to step onto the platform. He gazed across the valley to the distant mountain--blue with haze but sharply delineated against a pale sky--upon which the city rested. The space towers glittered, and lights flashed between them.

"What's wrong?" I said.

"Watch," Julian said. "We are not in the *Now*. This is yesterday."

I wasn't sure how, but I sensed Julian spoke accurately. The nanite-made *ai* growing in my brain had begun to grant me an intuitive sense of *when* we were in relation to the *natus* timeline.

A series of bright, blue lights flashed over the city, a score or more. Where each light flashed, a black, oval-shaped object had appeared and began to fall. Instantly the city erupted with a spray of lights, like scores of water hoses, throwing either tracer fire or other weapons I could not envision. Where the lines of light from the ground touched the falling objects, orange blooms sprang into being then disappeared again. And the objects in the air began to return fire, red and white tracers that burst from the objects like they were porcupines.

Something began to flicker over the city, becoming more pronounced with each touch of fire from one of the falling objects, a dome of pale light that absorbed the energy from above. A shield of some kind protected the city from the fire above.

But when the first falling oval reached the dome, it met no resistance. And once it passed through the dome, its fire began to impact within the city. More blooms of orange appeared within the city where the attacks struck. More fire impacted the dome, and it gradually grew more opaque, so that I could not see what happened within. More of the objects had fallen through the shield. I thought they might be bombs, and I waited for massive explosions to erupt, but none did.

"What are they?" I asked.

"Shen assault carriages," Julian said. "Each with five thousand troops. They are designed to teleport over the city beyond the range of the defense shield, and survive the fall into the target. Siola is lost, although the fighting will

163

continue in the streets and in the caves below for days to come."

Disappointment and sadness brushed my chest. Siola had been my first vision of a city of the future, and now it was being savaged. No, humans had not changed in a thousand years, had they?

"Why did they attack?" I asked.

"I told them to," Julian said.

I turned to him, clenching my fists. I resisted the urge to unpretty his face.

"It's a test," Julian continued. "They don't believe I and my family are not allied with the Alosians. They want to see if we act to stop or erase this."

"And will you?"

Julian gazed at him. "If my father Beran remained in control, we would not. He held our *neutrality* as sacred. Now I am in control. And I mean to humble the Shen."

"But not out of loyalty or patriotism," I said. "You are doing it just to further your power."

"You declaim truth," Julian said, his lips twitching into a faint smile. "While remaining purblind. But fear not: I will lead you to understanding."

I gave him a look filled with scorn.

Julian grabbed my arm. The dizzying effect of *peregrination* flipped me over, and I staggered as we landed. Then I realized where we were.

"What the hell?"

"I don't know where my sisters are," Julian said. "And they don't know where I am. But they know where you have been." He disappeared.

I turned with a growing sense of frustration and disappointment. I was home. In my apartment in Dallas. A thousand years in the past from where I'd been a moment ago. I stared around at the all-too-familiar place and pressed my lips together.

"Shit."

Catena 3

Tamara returned to the site chosen by Julian to be their parents' prison, a long-forgotten trojan asteroid in the Vaerdine-Lethiel orbit.

When she arrived, sensors detected her arrival and lighting panels in the ceiling snapped on. She swayed slightly as her body adjusted the barely perceptible coriolis force pulling at a right angle opposite the rotation. The asteroid had been sent into a tumble when humans first started mining it, to generate an artificial gravity close to one gee. The floor of the control center felt like a proper "down", but the asteroid wasn't large enough for people to comfortably ignore the sensation of an additional perpendicular tug every time they moved. Her nanites were already acting to counteract the sensation and neutralize the nausea and dizziness.

What Danny had told her still haunted her, and she had to make sure her parents were still alive. She passed her palm over the sensor beside the door to the mine. The tiny red light on it blinked once and ignored her.

"Dammit, Julian!" she shouted. The vapor of her breath began to crystallize before her eyes, but her voice only vibrated in her larynx as there was no atmosphere in the room to carry sound. She should not have done that, expelling the air in her lungs just to curse her brother. Now she had to work faster. The bitter cold and vacuum were already affecting her. Fortunately, her nanites were working to compensate, slowing her heart rate, shunting extra blood to her brain, even oxygenating her blood from the water in her body. That was a net loss of energy for her, though, which meant the nanites could not do it indefinitely. She only had a few minutes left.

She entered the override code she'd taken from Julian and the door slid open.

Julian had spent years fashioning this prison. Her elders stood, almost casually, in cylindrical columns of translucent crystal, as if they had been encased in ice. But their eyes were closed and they did not move.

Tamara regarded her mother's face, her short hair a mix of blonde and silver. She seemed frail, although she was easily as tough as any of them.

Next to Yana stood Arran, Tamara's father. His skin possessed the dark complexion of a native of Lethiel, but most of his hair had turned stark white. Tamara favored him in appearance, and as she gazed at him, she had a disjointed sense of staring into a mirror, and of seeing herself aged and lifeless. The sensation shook her and she turned away with a shiver.

Beyond her father stood tough, broad-shouldered Lerys, the wounds she inflicted still vivid in his flesh, and again her eyes filled with tears remembering his death.

Past Lerys stood a man Tamara had never been close to. None of them had. Eccentric, odd-looking Reys Andresen, the genius who had discovered time travel for the Alosians. His hair was white and tousled, and he sported a long white beard and thick white brows. His eyes were closed now, but she remember they were dark and always unfocused, because he always seemed to be pondering something else inside his head, even when he was addressing her directly.

He was the only one of the elder generation who had never fathered a child. He'd never married, and had disdained social and familial ties as obstacles to his work. But Beran and Lor, the other scientists, had admired him and respected him deeply.

Beyond Andresen stood the man most responsible for her current existence: Herol Beran, the Keyeran scientist who had raced Andresen to the discovery of time travel, then had used it to undo the damage the Alosians had done. Beran had a shriveled, decrepit appearance. He was the only one who actually looked *old*, because he was at least two hundred years older than any of the rest of the elders. His ugly face was swarthy and wrinkled, and his hair was a close-cropped iron grey. His hands and arms were also wrinkled and frail. The father of the oldest and youngest of them: Lor and Julian. Lor was devoted to him, but Julian detested him, just as Tamara had learned to detest him, the man who had dominated them and controlled them. It pleased her, and relieved her, to know he was dead, even though Julian had placed his body here with the others.

With the deaths of Lerys and Beran only three elders remained: her parents and Andresen.

Tamara stepped to the panel on her father's crystal. His vital signs were active but low. The crystal provided sustenance like an artificial placenta. The crystal was under a constant compression via the weight of the chamber on it, which generated a steady piezoelectric current strong enough to keep his *ai* dormant and power the life-support. It was a brilliant way to hold people who could *peregrinate* away with a conscious thought. She checked her mother's and then Andresen's cells. Well, they were still alive. Which meant Danny had been wrong. Relieved, she tried to *peregrinate* away.

Nothing happened.

For a moment she stood there, shocked. Then she used her *ai* to query the status of the control center. She suppressed the desire to shout a curse at Julian. A suppression field had been activated by her arrival. And worse, something, either deliberately or by accident, had pushed the asteroid out of its orbit. It was now on a trajectory that would spiral it into the sun in a few days. And she was trapped here, unable to jump away.

Shit.

She didn't have a way to correct the orbit. The station-keeping thrusters weren't strong enough. She wanted to scream at Julian; to hell with that, she wanted to kill the bastard. That's why he only pretended reluctance in giving her the coordinates. The little fucker. She loved him, but to him she was just another loose end.

She leaned against the control consoles and started to shake.

"Do something!" Danny said from behind her.

"What!" she demanded. "There is nothing to do."

"Tamara! This isn't you! You don't give up. You've never given up before! Don't do it now just because your brother fucked you over."

"You don't know me," she said. "I am two hundred and fifty years old."

"That's nice, granny." His words dripped with contempt. "Except I do know you. And you don't quit! Now find a way!"

"I don't know where to start." She thought she tried to sound piteous, to provoke sympathy in him.

"You could start by restoring life support to this piece-of-shit rock."

Life support? Yes. She was reaching the limits of her breathless endurance. She would die of asphyxiation long before it dove into the sun.

Oxygen generators. The control room had to have them when it was in operation. But this place was old, older than her family. The technology in it was beyond archaic.

Tamara searched her *ai* for information. Yes, the mine had used some of its rocks to generate oxygen. How? Oxides in the rocks used as the cathode in an electrochemical process, passing a current through the cathode and an anode of carbon in an electrolyte solution. Well, that wouldn't work. Any solution would have long ago evaporated unless it was well protected from the harsh vacuum when the place was abandoned. Maybe? It wouldn't hurt to try.

She found the master power switch for the console and turned it on. To her relief a myriad of lights came on instantly, some red and green, but most amber, many of them blinking as the system gave itself a series of power-on tests. She gave it a minute, wondering how many of the lights she could turn green by force of will.

The console went dark. She stared at it, her heart sinking. She flicked the master switch over and over. Nothing. The console was dead. And so was she.

Unless she found another way.

She spotted a tall cabinet with a faded red emergency decal on it. Inside were fire extinguishers, and a half-dozen silver canisters with attached hoses and masks. She pulled one out, but when she checked the pressure gauge it read empty.

Damn it!

She dropped it to the floor. There was no sound, but she felt a faint vibration through her feet as it hit and bounced away with eerie slowness. Each oxygen canister was empty, and she cast each away with greater and greater ferocity and anger. Finally, she grabbed the last one.

Empty.

Fuck!

Her shoulders slumped in spite of her growing resolve to find a way out.

Then she noticed a long grey metal box on the bottom shelf. She pulled it out. It had a flammable warning sticker on it. She opened it and found a single yellow cylinder, and in block letters on the side it read *Oxygen Candle*. She nearly laughed with relief. She set the cylinder upright, broke the seal on the cap, and opened it. She tore out the bright red activation tab, which ignited a powdered mixture of sodium chlorate and iron within. The cylinder grew hot rapidly, so she returned it to its metal box. She held her hand over the nozzle to reassure myself that a steady supply of oxygen was coming out, then she stepped to the door to the mine and entered the code to close it.

Nothing happened.

No!

Any oxygen would be lost into the mine and into space if she couldn't get this door closed.

She removed the mask from one of the empty canisters. She took the tube and pressed it into the mouth of the oxygen generator, but the pressure wasn't strong enough to force air into the canister. Damn.

Power.

She didn't have enough of it. Or... too much perhaps?

The console was dead, but the light panels in the ceiling were still lit. So where were they getting their power? From the same place as the dampening field?

She returned to the chamber where the bodies were being stored. She couldn't tell from the architecture of the cells, but it seemed reasonable.

Who first?

Beran. That way if she fucked it up he'd still be dead and she wouldn't regret any damage done to his body.

But as she studied the controls, her fury at Julian returned. The cells were powered from the weight of the ceiling itself on the crystal, generating a piezoelectric charge.

There was no off switch. It was not designed to be turned off. More proof that Julian had planned for this fate to be permanent.

Pressure. The crystal coffins were under constant pressure. They were bearing the weight of the ceiling. Which meant whatever has been bearing the weight before, Julian had removed. On either side of the coffins were piles of rubble, the broken natural or man-made columns that had stood here before.

Julian was impatient. It may have been his most critical flaw. So if he had broken the columns with a tool, he simply might have discarded it--there!

To one side of the nearest rubble pile lay a dark blue device in the shape of an arc about the length of her hand, and grooved so she could grip it. It was heavy, and had an inertia to it such that once it began moving in a direction, it took as much strength for her to stop it as it had taken to move it in the first place.

She recognized it; an archaic weapon Julian had liked to use called a *labrys*. It contained a dynamic quantum gyroscope that translated its angular momentum to the alpha field around it, momentarily pulling the interstices of the dynamic fields apart. She had never favored it. It was heavy, unwieldy, and messy when it struck, and required her to be too close to her opponent.

She raised it over her head, gripping it with both hands, and brought it swinging down with all her strength. Once it reached a threshold momentum, it began to leave a fleetingly visible trail in the empty vacuum around her like a wire heated to blue-white incandescence.

It struck the rubble and then cleaved into the stone floor with a sudden, silent shower of rock splinters and a cloud of dust. The abrupt transference of energy from its momentum to the field comprising the matter of the rock nearly wrenched it from her grasp. Faster than the human eye could follow the interstices of the fields recovered their tensors, obeying their own conservation laws of symmetry, proximity, and mapping. But the damage had been done, and a ragged fissure now gaped in the stone floor at her feet.

Angry triumph filled her. Now she could understand Julian's affection for this weapon. The satisfaction of using brute force complemented her fury so well that for a moment she stood there in the expanding dust cloud with a victorious grin on her face.

Fuck you, Julian. You tried to kill me and my parents. And now you have given me the weapon to make you pay for it, you little bastard.

The *labrys* was not a scalpel. It was not meant for fine work. She had to be careful not to injure her parents as she shattered the crystal columns around them. They were still unconscious, which was good, as waking up in vacuum being unable to *peregrinate* would have provoked panic.

She freed her mom first, then her dad. She hesitated, then rescued Andresen as his vital signs indicated he still lived. The cracks that started to appear in the ceiling told her she was pressing her luck now. If she tried to retrieve Lerys' and Beran's bodies, the entire chamber might collapse, and half the Family would cease to exist.

She used their clothes to tie the three elders together and dragged them to the mouth of the cavern. It was not a very dignified method, and again she was glad they were still unconscious. She reached the edge and peered down at the smoothed-out bore and the stars passing by as the asteroid tumbled. Tracks where carts used to carry ore to the entrance still radiated from the chasm.

She estimated the width of the tunnel. They would fall at one gee, but there would also be the centrifugal vector. Would it be enough to clear the edge before the tumbling asteroid collided with them? They'd have to fall about twenty meters to clear the lip of the hole. Her *ai* gave her a definite *maybe*. Damn!

Well, here's goes nothing. She grabbed the strips of clothing binding her elders to each other then shoved them over the edge, and their combined mass took her with them.

That had to be the longest two seconds of her life, but they cleared the edge of the bore and the rock spun away into the darkness of space. She pulled on the line to slow her tumbling and to get her closer to her family so she could be touching each of them.

Then she took them home.

Catena 2

I stood on the balcony of my apartment and stared up at the night sky, though there weren't many stars visible from within the city limits.

Who are you? I asked myself more than once. A backwater, prehistoric doctor? Everything you know is irrelevant now. You know the future. You know what is going to happen. You know that what you know now is nothing. You know as much as Neanderthals knew about medicine. Are you proud of your ignorance?

I thought about Tamara. I missed her. I ached for her. I wanted to take her into my arms and kiss her and hold her and love her. Sometimes it was Tamara with dark hair, sometimes it was with red hair, but it was always Tamara's face and body and spirit.

Damn. Am I crazy? I love a woman who is actually two different women from a thousand years in the future.

I dreamed of her. I needed her. I wanted her, yearned for her, and was haunted by her. And a part of me doubted I was worthy of her. I was a caveman, useless to someone like her.

But she has given me a glimpse of an incredible future, and I wanted to be a part of it, wanted to learn the myriad advances in medical science, wanted to learn the history of the human race for the next thousand years.

Being back here, back now, made me feel blindfolded in an art gallery.

I tried watching television and videos, but nothing held my interest. How could it? It was archaic. I tried to ponder the current political events in the world and how they would be viewed in a thousand years, and it was ludicrous. Who cared which political boundary moved, and which leader's pride had been wounded? The pettiness of it all sickened me.

I tried drinking myself senseless, but the nanites in my blood neutralized the alcohol. I shook my head in baffled amazement. I had become an anachronistic artifact. I was an alien in my own time. Damn Julian for bringing me back here!

I'd never felt entirely at peace here. I'd never had many close friends, and they had moved away. My family had their own paths. I'd had girlfriends, but had never felt satisfied.

But Tamara. I felt like a giddy high-schooler when I thought of her. Giddy and horny. I hadn't felt this lusty about a woman since I was a teen.

I sighed and returned inside. I sat at my desk in front of my computer and accessed the Internet. After a moment's thought, I searched for information about nanotechnology.

I began to read, and when I glanced up, it was morning outside. And to my surprise, the information resonated in my mind and didn't evaporate instantly. I realized that the rudimentary *ai* my nanites were building was now capable of storing the information I took in.

The prospect excited me. I stepped to my bookshelf, pulled out a book on popular physics and began to read.

When I looked up again, it was afternoon. With little effort, I could recall any fact from the book. It was not that I "knew" the information, just that I could recall it; or rather, my *ai* could. The data was being stored in a part of the *ai* called the *athenaeum*, the "library".

Filled with delight, I grabbed another book at random. I loved learning new things. My curiosity had always been insatiable. I'd chosen medicine as a career mainly because of the immense body of knowledge I was required to learn.

I took one of my old medical textbooks and began to read it, and saw the things that I'd forgotten or had misunderstood before.

I paused only to eat. The nanites demanded more energy from me than I was used to. Without their need, I would not have stopped for anything.

Except the return of Tamara.

My first indication was her scent, an earthy odor my thoughts identified even before it occurred to me to turn around.

She wore a grey jumpsuit that hugged her hips and breasts. Her short red hair was ruffled as if she had come out of a wind tunnel.

I dropped the book and surged to my feet. I kissed her, wrapping my arms around her, and she returned the embrace and kiss with wordless eagerness.

Afterward, as we lay in bed, I lay atop her and moved within her, and our eyes shared each other's souls, she said, "You are."

"As are you," I responded.

When I awoke it was daylight outside, and I thought I might have dreamed her return. But no. Her smell still clung to the bed, and to me. And something on the edge of my consciousness was able to give me the exact date and time, not like a voice or a clock, just an awareness, a knowledge that almost felt innate. It was just after noon, and in this timeline, it had only been a week since Tamara had first arrived in my emergency room bleeding and unconscious.

She stepped out of the bathroom wearing one of my shirts and nothing else. Her red hair was wet and brushed back from her forehead, clinging to her head like a skullcap. She smiled when she saw I was awake.

"Shower's free."

"Are we going somewhere?"

She gave me a wink.

I stood and put my hands on my hips.

"Fine," she said in a huff. "I am taking you to see my parents."

I nodded. "That's what I expected."

She gave me a skeptical frown. "You think you know me that well?"

"I do. I have a question, though."

"Yes?"

"It has been a week, here, since we met. But two weeks have passed for me. So am I still part of this timeline? If someone went back to kill baby Me, would I disappear?"

"No. *Peregrination* severed you from your *natus catena.*"

"And *catenae* are the linked chains of cause and effect?"

"Yes. Existence is nothing but the sum of *catenae* propagating through the *tau* field."

"And the *tau* field is time?"

"Yes."

"So… *peregrinating* severs your existing *catena* and forms a new one. And erasing my original *catena* doesn't affect me, but something that changes that *catena*," I spoke slowly to make sure I understood it, "without erasing it creates an *analogue* of me, because it no longer ends where it did before. It continues to propagate?"

Tamara's expression darkened at the word *analogue*, but she nodded.

"So I could go back and change my future enough so that I never met you, and then there would be two of me."

She frowned at me. "You could… "

"But why would I want to?" I pondered that. "A backup? A saved game point. But the one who stayed here and never met you wouldn't be me. I wouldn't have my experiences. I wouldn't have my consciousness. If I died, I would still be dead, even if I lived; it wouldn't help me. Unless…" I paused for a moment to articulate the thought. "Unless I brought me into the loop. Made me a part of the plan. A part of my life. Make me my… understudy? No, not the right word. My partner in crime? My right hand. So even if one of us bites it, the other is there to continue the big adventure."

Tamara gaped at me.

"Don't tell me you and your people never thought of that."

She shook her head. "We did. Of course we did. But that's as much a misuse of our technology as any other deliberate change to a timeline. So it was condemned by our elders."

"And the rebels? Your beloved Julian?"

She bristled. "What are you saying?"

"Julian is the poster child for throwing out the rules. I bet he has at least one *analogue* working with him, possibly more than one."

"No," she said, shaken. "It's not possible." But her expression indicated differently. "You don't realize the... psychological stress of meeting another you, a *you* equal in ego and conviction."

"I can only imagine," I said, taking her arms. "But you do know. How would Julian react?"

She pondered that. "I think... Julian--of any of us-- has the mental toughness to do that; he is hardheaded and not easily rattled. So yes, it's possible he has recruited his own *analogue*."

"Not just possible," I said. "I think it's almost certain."

I left her to consider that and went to take a shower. When I returned, she was again clad in her grey jumpsuit. I pulled on jeans and a black t-shirt. I stopped and glanced around.

"It occurs to me I may never see this place again."

Tamara frowned at me. "Are you feeling doomed?"

"Not at all. The opposite in fact. I'm just not sure when or if our travels will bring me back here."

"Our travels?"

I smiled at her. "I plan to be a part of your life for a long time to come, sweetheart."

She darted to me, crashed into me, pushed me to the bed and started kissing me. "You're good..." she said between kisses, "at saying... the right... thing!"

I held on to her and enjoyed the taste of her for a while.

"Ready?" she asked afterwards.

I retrieved the flechette gun Julian had given me, thrusting it into my back pocket. I nodded. She held out her hand and I took it.

My existence flipped and shuddered, but I tried to control my disorientation as our destination settled into place around us.

A deep, powerful orange light enveloped us, forcing me to squint. I stood on the edge of what appeared to be a Zen rock garden, a rectangular swathe of sand rippling like water from which boulders peaked like black icebergs.

The orange light came from a setting sun to my right, an impossibly huge, red-orange orb speckled with spots, half obscured by a distant, rolling horizon. The sky possessed the same orange hue as the sun.

I realized I stood in a very small section of a huge metropolis domed by a hexagonal lattice of clear glass. The city had to be at least ten kilometers in diameter. The landscape beyond the dome was as barren as the rock garden, and almost as beautiful.

"This is the planet Keyer," Tamara said. "This city is named Novoi."

"Sounds Russian."

She nodded. "Keyer was colonized during the Second Wave, mostly by European and African nations."

She led me to the cottage adjacent to the rock garden. It was a simple, unassuming structure made of a uniform white material I could not identify, neither brick nor stone nor wood. Some kind of plastic, perhaps, with a coarse texture. A pair of purple ferns in pots hung bracketed the door. A pair of rocking chairs sat on the porch to the left of the door. A black and white cat (I took a long look to verify that it was indeed a cat) lay on one of the chairs licking its paw.

Tamara led me to the kitchen. At the table in the kitchen sat three people, two men and a woman. They had been engaged in an animated conversation that Tamara's arrival interrupted.

The man who had been speaking was oddly angular, with a great deal of silver hair and a thick silver beard demanding attention of its own. His face was wrinkled and dark. He wore wrinkled clothes of a predominant khaki color. His appearance reminded me of images of old Karl Marx.

Doctor Reys Andresen. The discoverer of time travel.

The second man was dark and lean, with dark, simple clothing and pure white hair. His face was clean-shaven and smooth. His dark eyes regarded me with focused, stored energy. His facial features identified him immediately: Arran Decaire, Tamara's father.

Which meant the kind-faced, platinum-haired woman with fair skin and intelligent blue eyes was Yana Cartine, the Family's physician and the person I most wanted to have a conversation with.

Decaire said to Tamara, "Go."

Tamara nodded and disappeared.

"Where is she going?" I asked, trying to mask my resentment at the peremptory way Arran ordered her away.

"To find her sisters," Decaire answered, meeting my gaze. "And the abomination *analogue* she created."

"She is no abomination," I said.

"How can she not be?" Decaire asked. "A pretender to the identity of my daughter. A copy. A counterfeit."

I realized I had clenched my fists. "Have you met her sir? Or do you lack understanding of what an *analogue* is?"

Arran Decaire cocked his white brow. Andresen looked surprised. Yana bit her lip.

Yana said, with a stronger accent than Decaire's, "We understand *analogues*, Danny Nolan. Why would you think we do not?"

"Then you do not understand love," I said. I paused. I'd meant to say 'logic'.

"Love?" Decaire said with the faintest twist of his lips.

"Love," I repeated, straightening my shoulders. "You love your daughter. You love her today, you will love her tomorrow. And if the Tamara of today and the Tamara of yesterday stood here before you, you would not love them equally?"

"Love," Andresen said in a deep, accented voice. "Is a distraction. It is not principle."

"It is the foundation of principle," I said.

The wild-bearded old man shook his head, his expression hard. "Love undermines the foundation. It demands exceptions to the rules."

"And without it," Yana said. "Rules are empty of justification."

Her expression and Andresen's told me this was old ground for them. I appreciated her support. But I kept my gaze on Decaire.

He said, "Who are you, Danny Nolan?"

I smiled. "I am a fossil from the twenty-first century. Drawn into your mess." I was pleased to see amusement on Arran's face. "Because I helped your daughter, and then fell in love with her."

"Which her?" Decaire said.

"I fell in love with *her*," I said. "It is irrelevant that there are two of her now. I love her. Both of her."

"Yes," Decaire said drily. "For you it has become some kind of everyman fantasy. Two Tamaras for the price of one."

"No," I said. But I had to wonder how close that was to the truth. "No. I would never see her again if that's what it took to convince you to accept both as your daughter." Did I speak the truth? Did I really mean that? Never see her again? What would my life be without Tamara? Plain? Mundane?

185

Boring? Empty? Is that all she is? A source of entertainment? No! No. "I love her. I would give my life for her."

"Such may come to be," Arran Decaire said. "Are you truly willing to give yourself for Tamara? Give everything? Your life? Your identity? Your past?"

My identity? I wasn't sure what he meant. The only thing I was sure was that I loved Tamara and would do anything for her. "Anything."

Yana gazed at me with a ghost of a smile on her lips.

"Then have a seat," Decaire said.

I joined them at the table.

"Ask," Decaire said.

"Will you allow Tamara and her *analogue* to live in peace?"

"Of course," Decaire said. "She is my daughter. Do you think we would kill her, or coerce her into suicide?"

"But Sheyn..."

"Sheyn chose her own path," Andresen rumbled. "She possessed the insight to understand the perils of indulging in distractions. We can only hope the *analogue* Tamara holds such insight."

I frowned at him. "You mean you expect her to kill herself?"

Old Andresen regarded me without expression.

I shook my head with a contemptuous snort.

Andresen's eyes narrowed. "It is not your place to judge us. We play a role beyond your ken."

"I can judge you," I retorted. "And I will. I am human and that gives me the right. Julian is not wrong to oppose your goals and your methods."

"Our goals," Decaire said, "Have always been the same, to keep the *natus* timeline unperturbed. And our methods are not open to the grumbles of children."

"Even when your methods turn your children against you and make them hate you?"

"Even so," Andresen rumbled.

Yana's lips pressed together.

I said to Andresen, "You are a scientist." I looked at Decaire. "And you are a soldier turned scholar." To Yana, "And you are a physician. Yet together you make up a petty dictatorship as irrational and capricious as any autocracy."

Andresen laughed. "Irrational?" His expression filled with amazed scorn.

I suppressed my smile, pleased to get a rise out of the wild-bearded scientist.

Decaire stood. "Come with me, Danny." I followed him out of the house. We emerged into the orange light of the sunset. The older man waved me to a stone bench overlooking the rock garden. We sat and watched the rippling waves of the sand bathed in the orange light.

"Whoever chose to settle in this spot must have enjoyed sunsets and sunrises," Decaire said. "We are close to the north pole, and because of the axial tilt and the slow speed of rotation, this sunset will last about three months. Then it will fall below the horizon, and return six months later for an equally long and glorious sunrise."

"Are we in the *Now*?" I asked.

"No," Decaire said. "That would not be a wise place to be for people with enemies who can change time."

"I thought you had been captured by Julian."

"And Tamara rescued us. She didn't tell you?"

"Did she tell you she was working for him?"

Decaire nodded. "She told us. And she told us about you. She told me she loves you."

My heart jumped at that, and I felt myself flush. "I love her too."

I expected Decaire to say, caustically, "Which one?" Instead, the old man gazed out into the rock garden. "I know my daughter, and I know she will emerge from this stronger than ever. Both of her." A ghost of a smile played across his lips. "I am a sentimental man. And that part of me says two Tamaras is better than one because I will get twice the love in return. Who can object to that? But I am also a cold-hearted murderer. I've killed thousands of people. I can set my sentimentality aside when I have to. I require something of you, Danny Nolan."

My chest tightened at the expression on Decaire's face. "What?"

"I need you to betray us."

I stared at me. I waited for more explanation, but none came. "I don't understand."

"You will, when the time comes."

I peered at the white-haired man. "Do you know the future?"

"I wish I did!" Arran said with a sigh. "Who doesn't want the power to avoid devastating mistakes? The truth is, the only people with anything approaching foreknowledge are the Alphans."

"The machines?"

Decaire nodded, and there was a pleased glint in his eye. "The Alphans are better at identifying trends, weighing probabilities, and anticipating events than any other group. They don't forget. Every single iota is a data point for their calculations. I cannot tell you what is going to happen tomorrow, but a computer, given enough data, can give you an uncannily accurate prediction of what is likely to occur. This is why Alphans crave knowledge, data, the way humans crave wealthy, power, or pleasure. Are you aware of the paradox of the *Now*?"

I shook my head.

Decaire said, "We are not in the *Now*, but if we were, we could go no further. For all our technology, we have never been able to move ahead of the *Now*."

I frowned, rolling that around in my head. "Why?"

He shrugged. "Andresen, Beren, and Lor have been debating it for decades. To humans, the future has always been unknowable, as if it had not happened yet. That is just as true of someone from your century as it is of us. The future is, and always has been, inaccessible. Andresen believes the future exists only as a wave function that doesn't collapse until someone observes it."

I chuckled, and Decaire regarded me quizzically. "Sorry," I said. "That made me think of a popular analogy from my time. So we could call the idea Schrodinger's Future."

Arran smiled at that. "Amusing. It wouldn't amuse Andresen, though. Of course, nothing amuses Andresen."

I grinned.

"Beran and Lor oppose that interpretation. They both believe the Future already exists from Beginning to End as a deterministic series of causes and effects."

"*Catenae*," I said.

"Yes," Decaire said, nodding with approval. "The *catenae* are absolute, whether manifesting from the past or progressing into the future. Even standing in the *Now*, the sum total of *catenae* proceed inexorably into the future. According to Beran and Lor."

"Do you disagree?"

Arran shrugged. "I am not a scientist. I know demolitions, which use classical physics far more than Raslan field theory. It does not matter if the explosive are simple TNT or an alpha flux inducer; I know the yields, the necessary size and shapes of the charges, and where to place them." He stopped. "I am rambling like an old man. It has been a long time since I had someone new to speak to, someone I could trust."

I felt warmth at that, until I remembered Decaire's previous comment. *I need you to betray us.* What did that mean? Was he a secret sympathizer of the rebellious Younger Generation?

Tamara and Yana emerged from the house. I smiled at Tamara with the familiar flush of excitement. But I saw that now she appeared stressed and pallid. She smiled at me weakly and came to me for a kiss and hug.

"How long has it been?" I asked, studying her drained face.

Her lips twitched. "Just a couple of days."

"You look exhausted."

She leaned into me. "I am." Her voice was muffled by my shoulder.

"She can rest," Yana said. "Now it's our turn." She handed me a brown satchel.

Tamara grabbed me and kissed me fiercely. "Be well, Love." She said it in a formal sense that made me frown. "I won't be here when you return."

I caught my breath. "Why not?"

"I am sending her back to Julian," Decaire said. He met my glare with equanimity.

Tamara pulled me to her and kissed me again. "Don't worry, Love," she said. "I will find the information we need and we will stop him. Take care of my mother."

I could not help but chuckle at the absurdity of that, since Yana Cartine was easily as lean and fit as I was, and knew more than I did about, well, everything.

Tamara stepped back and Yana held out her hand to me. She too carried a satchel. Her hand was cold.

Catena 1

Every day, the *analogue* Tamara wondered where Danny was. It had been three days now since he had disappeared with the redheaded version of her. *The real me*, Tamara was always quick to remind herself. Why wouldn't he prefer her?

It had only been three days, but that was an eternity to a time traveler. Her imagination and self-doubt worked together to cast scenario after maddening scenario at her. Tamara feared he'd be an old man when she met him again, old and married for a lifetime to *her*. Or he had been turned by Julian. The thought of him suffering Julian's torture made her weep. But then, everything made her weep now.

Tamara felt helpless and useless, and only the need to protect her sisters kept her here in the city of the Shen, trying to convince Lao Ran Jun to ally with them, knowing that he had already allied with Julian. Today Tamara found herself in one of the Shangdu crèches, a nursery where the infants of the Shen were nursed.

The Cow Mother was a pale-skinned woman recumbent in a soft, overstuffed couch built to accommodate her contours. Two young female attendants sat on either side of the sofa, each holding an infant to her vast, ponderous breasts. The Cow Mother's mammaries were bigger than her torso, and rested on pillows of red silk. The babies simpered and suckled, and the attendants hummed to them as they fed.

Tamara watched the spectacle with fascinated revulsion. The Cow Mother showed no unhappiness. Her head had been shaved, and her face covered with a white powder and painted with makeup into a placidly beautiful mask. She beamed absently at the infants through half-closed eyes, although she might only barely be able to see them--and surely not reach them--past the unnatural masses of her bosom. Her beatific expression was one of serenity, rather than any particular fondness for the babes.

"Lady Tamara."

Tamara turned and bowed to Lao Ran Jun, the white-haired general who had masterminded the Shen's ascendency. He nodded to his guards, a pair of giants two and a half meters tall clad in ceramic lamellar armor, and they withdrew a dozen paces. They were Dragon Soldiers, and like the Cow Mother were fruits of meticulous Shen eugenics.

Lao Ran Jun said, "I would have more expected your sister Lady Alea here in the crèche, as she has long yearned for children of her own."

Lao Ran Jun liked to remind us how much he knew about us, although it no longer shocked us. Tamara was sure Julian had given him a full briefing on the Family. However, so far Lao Ran Jun did not know that we knew Julian had betrayed us to him.

A gong sounded. The attendants rose with the infants and bowed to the Cow Mother, who placed her hands on the heads of the babies in benediction. Then they left and four other women entered. These newcomers were dressed in nothing but black loincloths, and carried golden carafes.

Tamara said, "Recent events have made me reconsider the possibility of having children of my own someday."

The women circled the Cow Mother's couch and tilted their containers to pour oil onto her breasts. They set the containers down and proceeded to massage the Cow Mother, rubbing the oil onto her breasts and nipples. She sighed, smiled, and closed her eyes.

Lao Ran Jun cocked a white brow at her. "That would defy your family's tenets. Your parents had you sterilized just so a third generation of gods would not be born."

The Cow Mother's attendants missed no inch of her flesh, pouring out more oil for her torso, arms, hips and legs. They even helped her rise to oil and massage her back and buttocks. Nothing about the woman's body was oversized except her mammaries. Thousands like her filled the crèches of the Shen, selectively bred over scores of generations for breast size, and quality and quantity of milk. And disposition: any ambition or sense of self beyond their duty had been bred out of them. Tamara's empathy for them had congealed into a nauseating ball of pity in her gut.

"We are not gods, Lao Ran Jun," she said. "We simply possess technology."

"You control time," the white-haired man said. "You defy death. And you possess knowledge beyond the capacity of any other people."

Ah. He wanted information about the *sirdar*. He wanted to know how we are able to detect changes to the timeline. Julian had not told him everything.

The attendants settled the Cow Mother back on her couch, gently repositioning her breasts atop the red pillows, and the gong sounded. Another pair of young women brought more whimpering infants. They bowed to the Cow Mother, who welcomed them and blessed the babies. The babies' whimpers stopped as they latched onto the thick, dark nipples, and they began to suckle as the girls holding them hummed.

Lao Ran Jun waited for her to speak. He was used to dealing with Julian, who no doubt was glad to offer him information, and probably glad to brag as well. Instead, Tamara said, "Do you bring word of the Emperor's decision?"

This would annoy him on a couple of levels, because Tamara dodged the subject of the *sirdar*, and because they all knew he had not contacted the Emperor. He was the *de facto* ruler of the Shen, and his claim that he needed the Emperor's countenance to act was a mere delaying tactic.

He said, "I came to invite you to a performance this evening. The Emperor's Seventh Wife, her Royal Highness Li Lin Zha, has come to visit, and requested the entertainment." His tone suggested that the timing of this visit also annoyed him.

"Do you receive many royal visitations?" Tamara asked.

"Some."

"I am honored by your invitation, General. My sister and I will be pleased to attend the performance. Would it be

possible to meet the Lady Li Lin Zha?" Tamara asked
because it seemed to bother him.

"Of course," he answered. He bowed to her and
departed, and Tamara turned back to watch the babies suckle
at the generous nipples of the beatific Cow Mother.

Catena 5

Alea strode through one of the gardens of Shangdu. The strange, exotic plants fascinated her. Most of them looked like cacti, thick appendages radiating from a central point low to the ground, and covered not with spines but rough blue and purple scales. Each appendage bore a round fruit the size of her fist glowing with a pearly bioluminescence that filled the gardens with an ethereal radiance. Like everything else about the Shen, these plants had been produced by intensive selective breeding to produce sufficient oxygen and light for the underground caverns.

A young Shen girl clad in purple robes of silk moved through the garden. Her colors indicated she was a Plum Blossom girl. Her hair and low-key makeup were meticulously perfect. When she saw that Alea had seen her, she bowed, then approached and bowed again.

"How may I serve you, my lady?" Her voice was soft and accented, but her English was perfect.

"What is your name?" Alea asked.

"Wan Xiu, Lady," the girl said, keeping her eyes downcast.

"That means 'elegant'," Alea said with a smile. "You live up to your name, Wan Xiu."

"You are too kind, Lady," said the girl.

"What can I do for you, Wan Xiu?"

"Lady miscomprehends," the girl said. "I come to serve you, Lady."

Alea smiled. "How old are you, dear?"

"I have known seventy-three winters, Lady." She was older than Alea expected, about thirty Earth-years old. "You have been invited to attend a performance with the Lady Li Lin Zha this evening. The honorable Lord General Lao Ran Jun asked me to extend the invitation to you."

Something in the tone of the girl's voice made Alea extend the conversation. "Who is Lady Li Lin Zha?" She knew, or rather her *athenaeum* knew, and provided her with the information. But she sensed the girl wanted to say more.

"She is the Emperor's Seventh Wife. She arrived today to visit the Honorable Lord General."

"She and the general do not like each other?"

The girl gazed at her.

Alea smiled. "Please take me to her."

The Plum Blossom girl hesitated, then bowed fractionally and turned away. She led Alea into a series of caverns draped with scarlet silk. Jade statues of griffins crouched on either side of the entrance with fierce countenances.

Massive Dragon Soldiers armed with silver spears stood at the entrance. Wan Xiu spoke to them and bowed. One of the soldiers gave a barely perceptible nod and the girl led Alea into the chamber. More bright red silk draped the cave walls and hung from the ceiling.

Another Plum Blossom girl approached to meet them and bowed.

"The white devil woman seeks an audience with her highness the honorable Li Lin Zha," Wan Xiu said in the Shen language.

"The heavenly mistress has expressed an interest in meeting the white devils," answered the other girl in their soft, melodious language. "Why, I do not know. They are such ugly creatures."

Alea? Is that you?

Alea concealed her surprise at the voice in her head. *Kyren? Where have you been?*

Kyren broadcast amusement and delight. *I told you I would be back. I've been doing what I do best.*

What Kyren did best was go deep undercover, losing herself in roles and costumes to infiltrate the highest levels of their targets. Kyren loved to act and change her appearance, so she was a natural spy.

Alea peered at the two Plum Blossom girls, trying to see through their expressions and makeup, trying to see her sister underneath. But no, neither was tall enough to be Kyren.

The other girl turned and beckoned Alea, and she followed her into the next chamber, which in addition to red silk had bamboo paneling on the walls, rich rugs, and a large canopied bed. Next to the bed rested a glass and crystal table lined with gold, and before the table sat an intricately carved chair of red wood. The heavy smell of incense in the room was strong enough to make her eyes sting.

A beautiful Shen woman with alabaster skin, long, straight dark hair, and dark eyes sat in the chair. Behind her stood another Plum Blossom girl.

Alea surreptitiously studied both the girl and the seated woman as she came forward and bowed. "I am honored to meet you, most noble Highness Li Lin Zha."

The woman gave a slow nod and spoke in the Shen language, "What a frail, ugly creature this white devil is. I don't know what the Lord General is doing playing host to these people."

The girl behind her said in English, "The Honorable and Royal Lady Li Lin Zha bids you welcome and hopes the Lord General has proven to be a superlative host."

Well, Sister? Kyren's voice giggled in her mind. *What do you think?*

Alea stared at the girl behind the chair. Then she caught the eye of the seated woman.

Kyren! Alea said. *You are the emperor's wife?* "Thank you, Highness. Your words honor me. And the Lord General is a very gracious host."

Seventh wife. But his favorite. She giggled again in Alea's mind, though her face remained serene. Aloud, she said, "This white devil is well spoken, but it does not make up for her hideous appearance. How she bears to carry the weight of such ugliness, I do not know."

Kyren! Alea said. You left us only three days ago. Even as she said it, she knew that was an irrelevant comment. *How long have you been here?*

Twenty years, Kyren answered.

The Plum Blossom girl said, "The Honorable and Royal Lady Li Lin Zha thanks you for your kind words and compliments you on your exotic beauty. She also asks if there is anything else you desire to improve your visit with us."

Twenty years, Alea thought. She knew Kyren loved to immerse herself in her roles, but even for her twenty years seemed excessive. Alea had to reconcile the knowledge that the sister she had seen just a few days ago had aged twenty years in that time. Kyren must have sensed her shock.

This was important, Alea. And it's what I do best. Ask for a bath.

Well, that was true. Kyren was the consummate actress. No other member of the Family infiltrated as deeply as she did into whatever culture they were monitoring. But now it was not a matter of watching the Shen. It was a matter of the survival of the Family. It was a matter of manipulating and deceiving the Shen and controlling them to ensure that the Family survived the coup staged by Julian.

"If it pleases her royal ladyship," Alea said aloud. "I would like to have a bath."

"Ah," Kyren said in the Shen language. "This ugly devil realizes that she stinks enough to make the Ancestors weep. Tell her she has made a wise decision, and that I will join her. Wan Xiu, please inform the Honored Lord General."

The Plum Blossom with Alea hesitated only a barely perceptible beat then bowed and backed out of the chamber.

There! Kyren said. *I have sent his spy away for a time. Only my own girls I trust completely.* "Lien, please take the ugly barbarian to the bath chamber."

The girl who had been translating bowed to Alea and said "Please follow me, Honorable Lady."

The girl led Alea to a cavern filled with steam. The steam rose from an irregularly shaped basin in the floor of the cave. The girl helped her undress, and Alea slipped into the warm water with a happy sigh. The Plum Blossom girl brought a wooden plate with soap and washcloths.

The Lady Li Lin Zha entered a minute later, her black hair loose. The Plum Blossom girl assisted her in disrobing.

Alea tried to see her sister in this exotic woman. She was tall, yes, and Alea knew she could easily change her hair and eye color. She was thinner, and leaner. She had lost almost twenty kilograms of body weight since Alea had seen her last. Her thinness only enhanced the fullness of her breasts. No wonder she was the Emperor's favorite.

Lady Li slid into the water with a moan of pleasure. She didn't start bathing. She just sank into the water to her chin, her eyes closed, her long black hair floating and framing her alabaster face.

Being the Emperor's wife does have its perks, Kyren said. Now that sounded like Kyren.

Twenty years? Alea asked again.

Kyren kept her eyes closed but she smiled as she drifted in the hot water. *I bought a place as a Lotus Girl with a small house, and worked my way up to a Plum Blossom girl for Lord Wu Guan. From there it was easy to catch the Emperor's eye. Lao Ran Jun knows we are time travelers, so he would suspect anyone. He probably does still. But my position makes it difficult for him to assail me. And it gives me a position to make his life a little more difficult.*

She giggled again in Alea's mind. *Especially since I was making his life difficult long before he ever learned of us.*

We need to use Lao Ran Jun to lure Julian into a trap without either of them realizing what we are doing, Tamara said in both their minds.

Hello Big Sister, Kyren said gaily.

Kyren, Tamara said. *I am amazed how much effort you have put into this. And deeply grateful. You have done good, Little Sister.*

Kyren opened her eyes and exchanged a surprised look with Alea. Tamara had never been one to hand out compliments, and certainly not to Kyren. For most of their lives, they had only barely tolerated the other's presence.

So we are in a good position, Tamara said. *We know Julian talks to the general, but the general doesn't know we know. Yet. That will change the next time they meet, which could be at any time. We must be at that meeting. More importantly, we must take Julian at that meeting.*

He will be on his guard, Alea said.

Which is why we will attack from an unexpected direction, Tamara said. *Sisters, put our plans into motion. I will return in a day or so. Alea, tell Lao Ran Jun that I left to seek an ally.*

Tamara! Alea said. *You can't leave now. We need you.* Ice clutched her chest at the thought of Tamara leaving.

We understand, Tamara, Kyren said. *Go find him. Alea and I will handle the Old Dragon.*

Catena 1

Tamara felt as if she were drowning in her despair. It surrounded her and constantly threatened to overwhelm her and draw her under. Danny was with *her*. She'd either killed him or turned him. *Why wouldn't he prefer her to me?* She was the real Tamara. And she was damaged, which appealed to the doctor in him. He'd made his choice when he tackled her.

The thought wanted to crush Tamara, and she came close to weeping again. She thought about their time together at the cabin, where he'd paid no attention to anything except her. They'd loved and played and laughed as if they were on honeymoon. He'd opened up to her, telling her his secrets, and she had shared hers with him.

The last time she would ever be happy.

She went to his apartment door and rang the bell. Her hand shook, and her heart pounded in her chest. A sense of panic threatened to send her fleeing.

There was no answer. The lock was a simple mechanical one, so she had no problem opening it. She wasn't sure why she entered. If he wasn't there, she had no reason to be there. But she wanted to see his home. Nothing meaningful struck her until she entered the bedroom. Her heart sank.

The bed wasn't made. The positions and indentations of the pillows told her two people had slept here. And the faint scent of sex still lingered on the air.

For a moment, she thought she had to be in the wrong apartment. Until she found his security badge on the dresser. She clenched her fist over the plastic hard enough for her knuckles to turn white. She searched for signs of a woman's presence and found it on one of the white pillows. A strand of hair with a black root but dyed a bright red.

She sank to the bed, staring blindly through tear-filled eyes.

Cold emptiness enveloped her and seeped into her until she saw nothing and felt nothing except an inconsolable anguish, an inchoate helplessness, and a sense of finality that filler her with overwhelming sadness and regret.

So this is what an absolute absence of self-confidence felt like. Desolation. A cold, shaky emptiness. A suffocating vacuum. A constant, panicky sense of impending catastrophe. A sensitivity to every loud sound, every unexpected sight. Worse, a breathless anticipation of disaster in every form imaginable. And worse still, a smothering darkness permeating it all, filling every last corner of her mind, a voiceless null that beckoned her, urging her to a final embrace, a final letting go of struggles she could not overcome anyway. It was death that framed her waking mind now, framed it and saturated it and promised an end, a welcome end to the fear and the cold and the loneliness and the helplessness and the voiceless wails of terror and despair.

She thought about the Pond, the small black hole she visited when she sought absolute solitude. It seemed the black hole had settled itself into the center of her spirit and begun to consume her.

Strangely, that metaphor comforted her. Where had she left her skiff? Oh yeah, on Lethiel with Lerys.

You're crazy, she said to herself. Diving into a black hole won't help. You'll just slow down and have to endure this shit longer. Suicide requires a quick death. And death by black hole is the slowest possible.

It would be interesting though. To witness what actually happens beyond the event horizon. And the idea of a final embrace by the most powerful force in the universe was a little comforting.

Crazy woman, Danny growled.

The voice was so clear she jumped. But of course he wasn't there.

No, I'm not here. You really are going crazy, his voice said.

She sighed. Anger stirred in her gut, but the dark despair smothered it. She needed the numbness. It soothed the hurt. She had risked everything on his strength and presence, and now he was gone. He had chosen *her*. Or *she* had chosen him. Same difference. And why not? She was the strong one. She might have been broken by Julian, but she'd been reforged as well. She did her job and took what she wanted.

The way I used to be.

Her yearning for Danny, the ache to have him wrap his arms around her was so strong it took her breath away. Why had it come to this? A bitter, metallic taste of self-pity tinged her despair.

Why couldn't she return to an earlier moment and claim him for herself? It would make an *analogue*, but who cared at this point? Her and *analogue*-Danny could go back to our cabin in Yellowstone and live happily ever after.

206

But... her sisters needed her. She couldn't run away now. She couldn't hide, and she couldn't kill herself. Afterwards, yes. But not now.

She straightened her shoulders and stood. Instead of returning to her sisters in Shangdu, though, she chose a different destination.

She sought out the one person who she felt could help. Lerys. She arrived at his home on Lethiel and the gong sounded as she entered.

Her uncle rocked backward on his heels as she crashed into him and wrapped him with a desperate embrace. All the emotion poured out of her then and she wept. Lerys comforted her awkwardly. He had never been at ease with affection and social graces, but he held her and patted her back, and that was enough. He couldn't get a coherent answer from her, so he stopped trying until she'd settled down.

He led her to a chair at the kitchen table, then brought her a beer and a bowl of soup. She ate ravenously, drained the beer and accepted another one.

"You ready to tell her?" he said.

She wasn't. Now that she'd calmed down, she was terrified of how he would react. He might send her packing. She had come to do exactly what the Family had devoted centuries to prevent. The hypocrisy burned in her throat and nose and eyes.

Lerys gazed at her. "Something has happened. And since I haven't heard anything about it, I am going to start guessing you should not be here."

Tamara bit her lip. "No."

He regarded her. "Tell her nothing. I don't want to know. I will be a shoulder to cry on, but you will not turn me into an *analogue*. The future must play out as it will. Understood?"

Unwelcome tears again began to flow down her cheeks. She gazed at him through blurred eyes.

He regarded her, wavered, and then sighed. "Okay. Tell me."

She did.

Catena 3

Tamara Prime returned to Julian's residence on Luna in the *Now* to wait for him. She missed Danny already, and the wait drilled into her skull. She paced, she exercised, she ate, she slept fitfully, then woke to repeat the routine.

What if something had happened? What if Julian had attacked her parents again? What if Julian had found out their plan and moved against Yana and Danny while they worked to resuscitate Lerys and Beran? She still loved Julian, and shared his disdain for the Elders rules; she just didn't want him to hurt any other members of the Family.

She remembered an event from our childhood. Well, Julian's childhood. He had literally been a teenager; Paul had been in his twenties by then, and she was already over a hundred. Julian had fought with Paul over something petty, something to do with wrestling over a wine bottle. She had forgotten the actual argument, but Paul had goaded Julian into a naked rage. It may have been the only time she'd ever seen Julian truly furious. Paul had been a mean little snot and a bully, and had only just grown out of it. Paul's hellish behavior may have been the reason Beran had sterilized them, to keep the Family from producing any more anti-social scions.

Julian was already tall and strong, and despite his age had bested Paul in their melee. Julian had proceeded to beat Paul to a pulp with the very bottle they had fought over, and Tamara suspected if she had not intervened, he would have killed Paul then and there. Beren and Sheyn had come late to the fracas and proceeded to scold Julian, assuming he was the aggressor. Julian's stricken expression at the unjustness of their rebukes had moved me to take his hand and *peregrinate* to one of her favorite places, the 21st century and more specifically the Bronx Zoo.

He seemed to like it, and kept his seething emotions in check, but at one point, we saw a gorilla, a big black-haired mountain gorilla that sat on a rock in his confinement area and stared into space with expressive sadness while the humans murmured among themselves and pointed at him and tried to attract his attention. Julian had gazed at it for a moment, shaken, and then abruptly moved to a nearby bench. She followed and realized he had begun to weep. She sat and held him until the moment had passed. When he was himself again, he had regained his aloof, mocking attitude toward all of existence, including the gorilla.

They had never spoken of that day, but memory of it still made her throat tighten. That day had made Julian her special charge, and now she had to wonder what she had done wrong. Was he a sociopath, as Danny thought, or just an angry rebel? The fact that he had taken her and tortured her into a henchman confused her. His justification had seemed reasonable: she was the one most capable of stopping him. She was the one who had to be controlled and turned.

She loved Julian. Affection, yes, and sibling loyalty. But more. He was a tall, strong, and handsome man, virile and compelling. He had turned the heads of her and all her sisters at one time or another with his charisma and vitality. No one in her family had ever really talked about it, but the incest taboo had never been relevant to them. They were a group of energetic young adults filled with confidence, a sense of invincibility, and ardor.

In hindsight, it amazed her the Elders had been able to keep them restrained at all. For the older ones, Lor, herself, and Kyren to some degree, the sense of duty they had instilled still held. But the younger ones, particularly the youngest men, Paul and Julian, chafed at the rules. Perhaps it made sense that Beran had predicted a revolt, perhaps even foreseeing who would be its likely leaders.

Julian arrived. He appeared angry, but my reminiscences had softened me, and I went to him and embraced him with relief. He held her, momentarily surprised.

"I'm glad you're all right," she said.

Then she drew back and punched him. She had no doubt her blow landed and broke his nose, but he must have triggered his failsafe, because he moved as quickly as she did, ducking from her strike and catching her wrist in a painful grip. She tried to kick him in the balls, and in moving to avoid that, he weakened his grip and she wrenched her arm free.

"Bastard!" she spat at him. "Dumb ass! Ignorant little prick!"

When he realized she wasn't actually trying to kill him, he cocked his brow in amusement at her outburst. "You are correct on all counts."

"You tried to kill me and the Elders."

His expression changed. Not obviously, but it went flat. His amusement disappeared, and a guarded, practiced expression of insouciance emerged. "You went to the asteroid."

"Yes, and no-thanks-to-you I made it out alive."

He studied her, and there was a dangerous glint in his eyes that made her want to jump into a defensive posture. But she was committed to her course now. The only way to draw him out was to convince him she knew his secrets.

He said, "And the catafalques?"

Interesting way to refer to them. Did he mean the crystal columns themselves--as if they were dearer to him--or the bodies within?

"Destroyed," she said. "As you no doubt intended when you knocked the rock out of its orbit."

He regarded me. The threat behind his countenance did not lessen. His hand rose with deliberate casualness and clamped around her throat like a vise.

"Tamara. Sweetest of sisters, dearest of women. You know I adore you, more so than any other member of our Family. I would sincerely rue the need to end you." The way he said that, with his endearing blue eyes focused on her, and his expression devoid of emotion, crushed her.

He didn't mean it. He would gladly kill her, and looked forward to doing it. Only his belief that he still needed her protected her. The little brother she'd loved was gone, or subsumed within a twisted mind lost to its humanity.

Tears filled her eyes and rolled down her cheeks. He saw her stricken expression, and her tears, and released her abruptly, as if to avoid their touch. For a brief moment, he seemed confused, but he hid it quickly behind a scoff.

"You are the strongest of us. Why do you weep like a girl-child? For lost jailors and dictators who pretended the role of parents? They do not deserve your idiotic tears."

You do, she thought.

"Enough," he growled, waving his hand impatiently as if he meant to strike the tears from her face with force. He turned away, took a few steps, and then came back. "Control yourself, fool! Your weeping annoys me. We have tasks and you must compose yourself."

She swallowed against the tightness in her throat. "I love you, Little Brother." She might have indulged in her grief too long, because Julian frowned at her. Shit. It would only be that much harder to kill him if she tipped off her decision.

She stepped to him and began to kiss him, pressing against him with sensual craving. But he pushed her away. "Not now, Sweetest. We must go." There was a slight smirk on his face now. Make a man think he was desirable and you could get him to do anything.

"Where?" she asked.

"To retrieve your husband."

My heart jumped at that. "Danny?"

He gazed at me, frowning again.

She remembered that Danny was supposed to be here. "What have you done with him?" she hoped the alarm in her voice sounded sincere enough. She stepped toward him threateningly, a gesture she knew would amuse him.

He smiled. "Fear not, Sweetest. Your love is safe back in his natural time. He carries a message of truce from me to our sisters."

He caught her arm and we *peregrinated*.

We arrived at her father's cabin on Vaerdine. Fuck!

She drew the stun gun from her pocket and tried to shoot Julian in the back, but he had already disappeared. She whirled, falling into a crouch, waiting for him to reappear, but he did not. She shouted a curse.

She ran into the cabin.

"Danny!"

"Tamara?" Came the startled reply from the clinic downstairs.

She charged down and crashed into Danny, grateful when his strong arms caught me.

"We have to leave!" she said. "Now!"

He nodded and we entered the clinic.

Yana was there, as were the bodies of Lerys and Beran that she'd pulled from the asteroid. Holographic images hovered, superimposed over their bodies, and movement in the readouts embedded in those images indicated that Yana and Danny had succeeded in restoring life to them.

"Julian knows," she said. "We have to bug out." It was only a matter of time now--literally--before Julian destroyed this place.

"You cannot outrun *catenae*, Sweetest," Julian's voice said from behind her.

Danny drew his gun before she could shout a warning. With a bone rattling snap that made her ears ring, lightning flashed and struck Danny and he fell. A moment later the lightning struck her and numbing pain burst through her, erasing the futile, helpless rage.

She found herself staring up at the ceiling, the hand-driven nails and the manually carved rafters. Steps approached her; she felt them vibrating through the wood, growing nearer. A figure loomed over her. Julian.

He wore his usual mask of indifference as he gazed down at her.

"You have surprised me, Sweetest Sister. A part of me is proud of you. It is clear you are stronger and more resourceful than ever. It is small wonder the Fossil fell for you. What man would not?" He caressed her face and hair. "I have a simple question for you now, Sister."

Tamara closed her eyes and despair made her want to scream.

"What would you do to save the life of Danny Nolan?"

Catena 2

"Anything," I answered, glaring furiously at Julian. At least, I *tried* to look furious; my muscles, even those in my face, still stung from the electric shock.

"Right answer," Julian said with an insouciant wink. He began to pace again. I sat in one of the overstuffed chairs in Arran Decaire's cabin.

"So where is she?" I asked again. Tamara was gone when I woke up, and Julian wouldn't tell me where he had moved her. And my nascent *ai* had not recovered enough to call out to her.

"Answer me first," Julian said. "Where are Decaire and Andresen?"

One of Julian's soldiers came up the stairs and spoke to him in a language I didn't comprehend. It didn't even sound familiar. The man had a cool, earthy skin tone and sported dark hair, beard, and eyes. He was short and powerfully built. He wore a black jumpsuit with the symbol of a double-bladed axe in red on the shoulder. He carried a stun rifle, but held it awkwardly, as if it were a new weapon to me. To me he appeared more capable holding a sword or spear in his hand. Or a club. His brow ridges and chin definitely seemed prominent.

Julian issued an order and the man nodded and left.

I said, "Did you recruit cavemen?"

Julian hit me with a scrutinizing stare. "No," he finally said. "But close."

"How close?"

Julian gave a ghost of a smile. He sighed and sat in the chair next to me and stretched his long legs out. He leaned my head back and closed his eyes. "I'm tired," he murmured. "I can't even remember how long it has been since I slept."

"Your conscience keeping you awake?" I asked. My hands clenched and unclenched. I had to resist the urge to pounce on Julian and strangle him. I was unbound; Julian hadn't bothered to restrain me.

Julian chuckled but did not open his eyes.

I said, "What have you done with Yana and the bodies?"

"I placed them back into stasis. Not as good as the catafalques I'd built on the asteroid, but adequate enough to keep them down until this is over. And I think it will be over soon. Did my other sisters make contact?"

"No," I said. "I was there for only a few days, then Tamara found me."

"And then?"

I remembered the lusty reunion and was glad Julian wasn't watching my face. "Then she took me to meet her parents."

"Where?"

I smiled to myself.

Julian said, "I need to return you to your own time. So they can find you."

"No," I said almost instinctively. "I don't want to go back there." Being there had made me feel trapped and blind.

"It is necessary," Julian said. "Else they can't find you."

"You did."

Julian chuckled. "I cheated."

I frowned. "How *did* you find me?"

Julian didn't answer, but there was a smirk on his lips.

Catena 2

Something went wrong.

I had tried to jump to Tamara's place on Alpha Luna.

Julian had left me in his original time, but I had quickly started to go mad. I hated the idea that the Family members were fighting for their survival against Julian in the future, and I was stuck in the past feeling useless.

So I had come up with the idea of going to the Alphans for help. At first I wasn't sure what I could offer them for their assistance. Then I remembered my conversation with Arran Decaire and realized I did have something to offer.

But my attempt to *peregrinate* to Alpha Luna did not go as planned.

I found himself standing in a small white cube of a room, barely ten feet square. Had I landed myself in prison? Had Julian sabotaged my *ai*?

The walls went out, plunging me into darkness. There had been no visible source of light except the material of the empty cube itself.

A voice devoid of emotion and gender, originating from no apparent source, said, "Who are you?" Then a deep, reverberating male voice repeated, "Who are you?" Immediately it was followed by a female's gentle contralto: "Who are you?"

"I am I Nolan," I said. His voice fell flat, as if I stood in an area of immense nothingness.

"Insufficient data," said the female voice.

Undoubtedly true. I felt relief flow through me. Well, they-she-it certainly sounded mechanical. "Daniel Peter Nolan. Born January third, 1986 in Dallas, Texas. Social security num-"

"Danny Nolan," said the female voice. "A member of the group known as the Family. Also known as the Guardians of Time."

"Uh… well… yeah?"

"We estimate a sixty-six percent chance you have come to seek assistance against Julian Beran."

I was taken aback. "You know?"

"We estimate a sixty-nine percent chance Julian Beran is engaged in taking control of the group designating itself the 'Guardians of Time.'

"He is," I said. "So call it a hundred percent now."

Silence.

"Are you recalculating your probabilities?"

Silence.

"Hello?"

The silence began to disorient me. I had no sense of touch or smell or up and down. I had no visual cue to anchor myself, no aural cue to orient me.

"Ask" said the disembodied voice.

"Yes," I said. "Yes, of course I want your help."

And more of the damned silence.

"You know why I'm here," I said. "You have no doubt predicted exactly why I am here."

"We have."

I pursed his lips. "Coy bastards, aren't you." My resentment was more than half directed at myself. Embarrassed guilt gnawed at me, even though I believed this is what Arran had meant for me to do.

I'd come here to offer myself as an informant, a source of data for the Alphans that would give them the power to do what the Family could not: predict the future. Did they foresee that? Is it possible they knew what I meant to offer before I ever spoke? That kind of capacity to know the future was frightening.

"Make your offer," said the disembodied female voice.

I cleared my throat. "I believe that the thing you desire most is data, to strengthen your capability to forecast the future. I offer myself as a source—"

"We accept," said the voice. "We will assist you against Julian Beran and you will report to us regularly. You will not, of course, reveal this arrangement to anyone else."

And there it was. I'd known about the Guardians for only a few days, and now I was offering to be a mole against them.

A glowing green handprint appeared in the wall before me. I stared at it suspiciously. "What is this?"

"The weapon you need."

I reached out to place his hand on the imprint but stopped.

"Okay," I said. "O masters of forecasting. What is my probability of success?"

"Fifty-nine percent," said the voice. "With an error factor of three percent."

That low? "Is there a way to improve those odds?"

No answer.

Shit.

"What is the nature of this weapon?" No answer. I pursed his lips. "I'm not doing this without information."

"Nanites," said the voice.

I waited for more explanation, but none came. "You want to turn me into a disease vector?" The idea twisted in my gut. "Would these nanites harm anyone except Julian Beran?"

The silence grew heavy and oppressive.

To hell with this. As far as I knew, the Alphans might be asking me to introduce a virus that would kill all the Guardians, including Tamara. "Not gonna happen."

"The nanites are not contagious," said the voice. "Except via your touch."

My touch? So I will decide who lives and dies. The sick feeling in my gut deepened.

"And if I do not do this?"

"Alpha will act against the Guardians and eliminate all of them."

Ah.

Alea had said humanity was fortunate the Alphans lacked human emotions like anger, ambition, or pride. But they did possess a drive for self-preservation.

Could I become an assassin? I was a doctor. How could I become a killer? In self-defense, yes, but deliberately reaching out to touch a victim in order to take his life? Would it feel less like murder if it were, somehow, in self-defense?

"I have a counter offer," I said. "Give me a weapon. A gun. A flechette gun. With darts filled with the toxic nanites. Then I would be glad to shoot the bastard." *I think.*

"This would lessen the chance of success," came the emotionless response. "To fifty-one percent."

"Even odds," I said. "If I fail, you can always put your backup plan in motion. I'm sure you have one. And you get a hundred percent chance of my cooperation with this one."

No answer. The silence grew heavy, then oppressive, and still the Alphans did not respond.

***

I gazed across a grey-green sprawl of sparse grassland that seemed to cover the entire world, shivering in a steady, bitter north wind. My *ai* told me this was Dallas, and the time was *Now.*

I had given in to the urge to see Earth, the Earth of the *Now*. It had changed. Immensely more crowded, with fifty billion people, most living in a vast, unbroken urban belt along the equator huddled between huge ice sheets.

But my city had ceased to exist. I didn't see a single tree in his field of view. All the vegetation had died, along with the old city I'd known, under a five-kilometer layer of ash and tephra from an eruption of the Yellowstone caldera three hundred years ago. The ash had buried a quarter of North America. The eruption had plunged the planet into a winter that lasted twenty years and triggered a new ice age that had yet to end.

I recognized nothing in the geography around me. The only certainty of my location came from my *ai*. For a moment, I thought the *ai* had malfunctioned, even though I knew I would not see anything except grassland. Knowing what to expect was different from really seeing it. I felt as if I'd been punched in the gut. My past, my origins, my family, any possible clue or landmark or hint had been effaced. I couldn't reconcile the memory and the reality.

I'd expected some sense of comfort from coming here. But there was no feeling of home here. No reassurance. No pleasant nostalgic warmth. Too much time had passed. Too much had changed. A thousand years later, I was a man without a home.

I could return to my century of origin, make myself fabulously wealthy with my foreknowledge. Wealthy and powerful. Yet it didn't appeal to me at all. All I had left was a forgotten past, an unknown future, and the *Now*.

Something moved on the edge of my vision. I peered in that direction, but all I saw were tundra sedges shivering in the bitter wind. I saw movement again and caught sight of a bright, amber-colored eye regarded me through the shifting grasses.

A cougar. A big one. Tawny colored, with beautiful yellow eyes that watched me intently. Its ears were flattened and it moved slowly, working itself closer to a point from which it could pounce on me.

Adrenaline flowed into my veins like ice water and my heart pounded. I drew my pistol, but I didn't want to use it. The cougar was a fantastic specimen. Its species had grown in the last millennium, longer and more muscular, bigger than any version I'd ever seen in a zoo. With the retreat of humanity from the northern latitudes, it had no doubt benefitted from its new status as an apex predator.

Well, I was finished here anyway. I had come to regard my old home and found the journey unsatisfying. No reason to stay long enough to give the cat the chance for a meal.

It sprang, bounding toward me with an economy of motion that I almost paused to admire. I activated my *ai*. A d'Alembert field enveloped me and I was swept from my inertial frame of reference and hurled through the interstices of the dynamic fields that gave reality its form.

Amil Raslan was the first to propose that the underlying structures of existence were fields, not particles, said Reys Andresen's dry, accented voice. *Particles are merely the results of field interactions. Matter is made up of atoms, yes, and atoms of sub-atomic particles. But the particles are only projections into the time-space continuum of the interstices of the thirteen dynamic fields.*

I staggered with a disorientation I would never get used to as I arrived at my new location. Or rather a now familiar location. The white cube of the Alphans.

"Okay," I said aloud. "Where did I go?"

The female voice answered, "We estimate a sixty-eight percent chance that you went to Earth." It paused a fraction of a moment. "Of the current time. In the geographic region you once called Dallas."

In spite of myself, that surprised me. And reassured me. Yes, these Alphans were good at predictions. Giving them a better grasp of the future than the time-travelers.

"Okay," I said. "I am convinced. Now what?"

"There is a seventy-seven percent chance Alea Eril, Kyren Cartine, and the analogue of Tamara Decaire are in Shangdu currently negotiating an alliance with Lao Ran Jun in order to capture or kill Julian Beran. We estimate a sixty percent chance Julian will spring their trap, but only a nineteen percent chance they will succeed. If you are there armed with the weapon we have given you, the chances of Julian being killed or captured rises to sixty percent."

"And what is the second most probable event?"

"A twenty-one percent chance he escapes with injuries, and a nine percent chance he escapes uninjured."

"And the chance of me or one of the girls getting killed?"

"We see a twenty-seven percent chance one of you will be terminated, independent of other outcomes."

I grimaced. "Okay."

"We remind you of your obligation to us."

"I know," I said with a bitter taste. "I work for you now. Any last advice before I go?"

The voice did not answer.

"Right." I looked into my *ai* and triggered the coordinates of my destination.

Catena 6

Kyren returned to her chambers and her Plum Blossom girls pampered her with an oil and powder massage. They dressed her in cool silk robes and brushed out her hair until it gleamed. Then they reapplied makeup to her face. Finally she was ready for her afternoon assignation.

"Lady," her girl Chan said. "Lord Shu Wen is here."

Kyren smiled inwardly in anticipation. Shu Wen had been one of her favorites for a few years now. The young officer was a member of Lao Ran Jun's general staff, and chief of resource outlay. Thus, when she came to Shangdu he was always the first to visit her to determine how much her holiday was going to cost the Old Man. He was young to his position, confident, virile, and potent, and it had been easy to seduce him and even let him think it had been his idea. Their trysts were ardent and their pillow talk priceless for both of them. She did not doubt that he reported the information to the Old Man, so she was sure to give him plenty of salacious and incriminating tidbits about various people at court, particularly those who opposed Lao Ran Jun's policies. And so she was able to glean her own information about the state of affairs in Shangdu and the military.

Shu Wen entered the chamber, handsome in a crisp black uniform, his face an emotionless mask. He bowed to her. "We are honored by your presence, Royal Lady. Our ancestors smile at your arrival."

She responded with her own ritual platitudes, not letting her inward frown show on her face. Shu Wen was angry about something. There was a flatness to his dark eyes, a lack of movement in the creases of his face that betrayed an effort to control inner turmoil. His focus was elsewhere. Now she was even more interested in getting him alone, to probe him while he probed her. After a few minutes of small talk, she extended her ritual offer to share tea with him in her bedchamber.

He followed her into the room, and sat at the small crystal table. She dismissed all but one of her Plum Blossom girls, Chan, who poured steaming tea from a silver carafe into ceramic cups for them. Chan then bowed and withdrew to a distant corner of the room out of earshot. She remained to act as a nominal chaperone, to satisfy the conventions of propriety and honor, but Kyren trusted her, and she politely turned from them to attend to a project of her own.

Kyren stepped to the officer and kissed him, wrapping her arms around him. He returned her embrace and kiss, a deep, long kiss that left her breathless.

"I have missed you, my love," she said as he kissed her neck.

"And I you," he said with soft gruffness.

She rubbed his shoulders, feeling the hardness of muscle and bone, and the heat of his life passed through her silk robe and warmed her breasts and abdomen.

She stepped away, breaking contact completely. He cocked his head, regarding her.

His emotional chaos was even more palpable now. She gazed into his eyes and saw only a hard flatness that confused her. If he'd taken a new lover and meant to end it with her, she would expect to see guilt, regret, or sadness. If it was a breakup he desired himself, he would show eagerness, or anticipation, or relief. But he showed only a well hidden anger, which meant he suffered from a storm deep inside. She had never seen him so detached, and in a society that treasured detachment.

And he tasted... different. His taste had always been strong and sharp, an extension of his nature. But now. Her mind groped for a word to put to it. Now he tasted... plastic.

"What is wrong, my lord?" she said in a formal tone.

"Nothing, my lady," he answered. An undercurrent in his voice betrayed the anger, even the rage he kept bottled up. He hesitated. "I have been... ill recently."

"Ill?"

"I am told it was shāo rè fever."

She'd heard nothing about him being sick, especially from an illness often terminal among the Shen. But it's possible it had been kept secret. Could it explain this fury storming through him? Now she felt bad for pulling away so fast. She moved back into his embrace contritely.

"Are you recovered, my love?" she asked.

He smiled at her, almost perfectly insincere. "Mostly. Your ministrations ought to complete my recovery." He began to kiss her again.

They helped each other out of their garments and moved to the bed, but their lovemaking left them both unsatisfied. Instead of familiar partners, it felt like the awkward fumbling of inexperienced youth. His reactions, his touches, his every response felt *off*. In the end they lay recumbent and quiet.

The attack, when it came, was so subtle she did not immediately recognize it. The toxin moved through her bloodstream and her nanites detected it, but did not react to it at first. They did not recognize it, and so far, it was doing no damage. Only when the poison crossed the blood-brain barrier did the nanites begin to attack it. And it attacked back, killing the nanites as it died. A sense of pressure, a sudden onset of headache was her first warning. She queried her *ai* and discovered the attack.

She sat up. "What did you--?"

He watched her.

She moved to climb out of the bed, but he caught her arm and pulled her to him and wrapped her in a powerful embrace. Extraordinarily powerful.

She was not a weak woman. Her nanites kept her muscles toned to a level beyond most humans. But she felt as if his arms had turned into carbynet beams, utterly unyielding. She struggled, trying to squirm out, but his hold tightened, not hard enough to damage her, but enough to pin her to him.

She stared into his eyes, and this time he did not try to hide the hostility and malice behind his mild expression.

She *peregrinated* to the center of the room.

He sat up. "You are not," he said. "Who you appear to be." His tone was cool.

"Neither are you!" Kyren said. "Chan!" The Plum Blossom girl at the far end of the room jumped up, startled. "Shu Wen is an imposter. Warn the Lord General."

The girl hesitated as he turned to her. Then she ran for the door. He gestured, a flick of his hand so quick Kyren couldn't follow it, and three tiny holes appeared in Chan's purple robe. She fell, crashing against the door.

Kyren cried out and ran to Chan's body. Her robe was darkening, and the smell of death rose from her now. Kyren sobbed, shaking the body. Hot tears scored her face and she brushed Chan's lustrous hair as a storm of disbelief and grief filled her. Chan had been her closest friend, closer than either of her sisters had ever been.

She said in a choked voice, "I will destroy you for this."

"Unlikely," said the imposter. He climbed from the bed. "Who are you? You teleported without a platform or beacon. That technology does not exist. Yet." His eyes scanned her and the room as he approached her.

Kyren *peregrinated* behind him. Lerys had trained her well, and her blow would have broken the neck of a normal man. But it felt as if she'd struck a statue. She gasped in pain as her numb arm fell to her side. He turned to her with such speed he blurred before her eyes. He caught her throat with his hand in an inhumanly strong grip. But he didn't squeeze. He held her there and stared into her eyes.

"Pulse," he said. "Breath." In another blurred motion, the finger of his free hand slashed across her face, leaving a stinging pain then a lingering tickle. "Blood. Tears. You seem human."

"You don't," she said. But he did, and that is what disturbed her. His skin felt normal, so had his lovemaking. He breathed. He had a pulse. Only his taste had been off, and the flatness of his eyes hiding a roiling chaos of dark emotion, and his preternatural strength and speed. "What are you?"

He continued to stare at her. He said in English, "You are one of the Guardians?" She didn't answer, and did not let her consternation show on her face. But he said, "Your pulse has quickened, and your blood pressure has increased. And the increased warmth in your skin indicates that I have spoken accurately."

How could he know that? What but a machine could detect such faint signals? "Are you Alphan?"

The rage that flickered in his dark eyes surprised her, and his grip tightened enough to hurt. A slightly contemptuous crease appeared on the corner of his lip. "I am not Alphan. I am better in every way to the Alphans."

He changed before her eyes. His flesh seemed to crawl with a life of its own and take a new shape. His hair grew out, lengthened and straightening. Breasts filled out on his chest, the nipples widening and thickening. His external genitals disappeared, absorbed by his body, and his hips widened. He grew a few inches taller as his nose changed shape, his eyes narrowed, and his lips grew fuller. The change was not immediate. It was slow enough for her to watch it, fascinated in spite of herself. And while it was happening, he was focused on it. He held her without paying attention to her.

Finally it was done and Kyren stared at a duplicate of herself, even to the faint freckles on her left cheek and the mole in front of her right ear.

The imposter said, in Kyren's voice, "How long have you been impersonating Li Lin Zha?

"I have always been Li Lin Zha," Kyren said, and was rewarded by the puzzled crease on the imposter's forehead. "How did you do that?" She scanned her *ai* for data on the kind of technology demonstrated. Centuries ago metamaterials had been used to replace flesh and bone to increase life spans. One of the capabilities of such bodies had been a rudimentary ability to change their shapes. What had those people called themselves? "*Jinins.*"

The imposter snapped her neck with a flick of his wrist.

Kyren's fail-safe activated when it detected the severing of her spinal cord, and abruptly she moved six seconds into the past, to the point before he killed her. She *peregrinated* to the other side of the room, reeling from the disorientation. From his perspective, she simply moved faster than his decision to kill her.

He turned to her. Or she turned to herself. Seeing an exact duplicate of herself unsettled her. "Are you Jinin? Or, rather, a descendent of the Jinins who perfected their shape changing? Since we have heard nothing about you for centuries, your people have done a good job of keeping yourselves concealed."

"As have you," said her doppelganger.

"We don't have to be enemies," Kyren said. "We are both here to watch the Shen."

He shot her. She saw no gun, but his hand rose in a blur and the impact in her chest knocked the breath out of her. She gaped at him for a moment before she lost consciousness.

Her failsafe brought her back to just before he raised his hand. Again, from his perspective, she simply moved faster than he did. She jumped to Alea's room. Her sister looked up, startled.

"Shu Wen is an imposter. I think he is Protean."

Alea frowned. "A shape shifter?"

Kyren told her what happened.

Alea pondered that. "Letting him continue places you in danger."

"And killing him would make the Old Man suspicious."

"If we can kill him. We need something to penetrate an engineered anatomy."

"He still has a human brain and nervous system. At least, the Proteans of centuries ago did."

"We have to assume that their most vulnerable features are also the best protected."

"Do we go to Lao Ran Jun?"

Kyren pursed her lips. "Well, he has weapons we do not. I hate the idea of ruining my identity but what can we do?"

Kyren pulled on one of Alea's robes provided by their hosts, then the two of them walked to the Old Man's residence.

But Lao Ran Jun was already on his way to them with dragon soldiers. With him strode Shu Wen clad in his crisp uniform. The Old Man snapped an order and the soldiers surrounded the two women, their spears glinting in the light of the bioluminescent orbs.

Catena 5

Alea squinted at the sudden flood of light into her dark cell.

They're here, she said to Kyren.

Don't worry little sister. You know they can't hurt you, Kyren answered in her mind. The Old Man had separated them, though he probably suspected that they could communicate via *ai*. Julian might also have told him that Alea was the weakest of them, that she feared isolation and darkness.

"Why have you not escaped?" Lao Ran Jun asked. "I know you have the power."

"Because we seek an alliance with you," Alea answered, her throat dry. "To show you we are not your enemies."

"Yet you spy on me."

"Of course," Alea said. "As do the Proteans."

The old man frowned at her. "Your sister makes the same claim. But I have known Shu Wen for years. He denies the charge and I believe him."

"And you knew Lin Li Zha for many more years."

Lao Ran Jun said, "I cannot believe she never existed, that she was always a spy."

Alea smiled. "We are time travelers."

The old man harrumphed. "Who do not care about giving twenty years of your lives. Are you immortal as well?"

Alea thought of her mother and said, "We are not immortal."

Lao Ran Jun regarded her. "You and your people confuse me. Strength with vulnerability. Capability with ineffectiveness. I think it might be best to simply exterminate you."

Alea stifled a shiver. "You could not," she said, trying to radiate bravado.

The Old Man smiled slightly. "Perhaps. But it remains true you can move at will through space and time. So why are you here?"

"We seek your alliance," Alea repeated.

He gazed at her. "How would you prove to me that Shu Wen is an imposter."

"Summon him," Alea said. "And punch him in the jaw."

He frowned at her. "Make me trust you."

Alea bit her lip. "How?"

"Tell me how to kill you."

She stared at him. "I don't want to die."

He said, "Upon the honor and probation of my honored ancestors, I will never reveal the information you tell me, nor will I use it against you or your family."

She sighed. "I can't tell you."

"Then I cannot ally with you. You are unwilling to trust me, so I am unwilling to trust you." He turned to leave, and Alea bowed her head, thinking he was leaving her alone again.

But he stopped.

She peered up at him.

He came to her and crouched before her. Now she could see his face clearly, and more importantly the hostility that raged behind his eyes. "You are a mystery to me. A legend come to life. I will do what I must to learn how to destroy you."

It is the Protean, Alea said to Kyren.

Get out! Kyren shouted in her mind. He'll kill you, Alea! Come to me!

His hand moved so quickly it was a blur. He struck Alea and she slumped, unconscious.

Catena 7

Lao Ran Jun stood in his bedchamber. The sudden appearance of the Lady Li Lin Zha, the imposter, startled him. She took his arm.

The *peregrination* buffeted his equilibrium, but he recognized the cell where Alea was being kept. The girl lay slumped against the wall, unconscious and bloody. To his astonishment, he found himself staring at himself in full uniform, standing over her.

His double looked up, startled at their arrival in the small cell. Then, swiftly, he raised his hand toward the Old Man. Lao Ran Jun rocked back on his heels as flechette darts slammed into his chest. He glanced down at the spreading blood on his chest, then the sudden drop on his blood pressure rendered him unconscious.

Dizziness swept over him as his fail safe, the device given him as a gesture of good faith by Julian Beran, shifted him back in time six seconds, just enough for him to *peregrinate* to the other side of the cell and let the flechettes burst into the wall where he had stood.

His duplicate turned to gape at him. "You are one of them! You!" His expression moved from baffled fury to wariness. He stooped, grabbed Alea by the neck, and lifted her off her feet where she dangled like a rag doll.

Kyren froze.

The Protean regarded her. "Is that it, then? Your ability is confined to conscious thought? How disappointing." His hand flexed and snapped her neck.

Kyren jumped to the Protean's side just as Alea's failsafe bounced her back the six seconds. Again, to the Protean, it appeared that they just moved more quickly than he did. Kyren caught Alea's waist and jumped away, leaving the Protean and Lao Ran Jun staring at each other.

"You are revealed," the Old Man said to the imposter image of himself. "I will do what is necessary to drive you and your kind from your hidden places among my people. Your secrecy is no more."

The Protean's lips twisted in contempt. "Then I shall destroy you and your kind first."

"We already know that is impossible," the Old Man said.

The Protean's face radiated poorly concealed rage. "I will make it my duty to destroy the Shen for this. You will watch your civilization fall into ruin and shed impotent tears as I eradicate your people." He turned and left the cell.

Lao Ran Jun stepped to the intercom and raised the alarm. He ordered a full mobilization to guard all the teleporter platforms in the city, and allow no one access for any reason.

Then he hurried after the imposter. The Protean moved directly to the nearest teleporter. The guards were taken aback by the arrival of their Lord General, and they almost allowed him to step onto the circle. But Lao Ran Jun reached the chamber and shouted

"Arrest him. He is an imposter."

The Protean moved with impossible speed and fought with impossible strength. He shrugged off wounds that should have killed him. He bled, but not enough to slow him. He darted around the soldiers, struck blows with his fist that dropped men twice his mass.

Handfuls of soldiers tried to tackle him and pull him to the ground, but he flung them off like toys. Thunder weapons detonated and gaping wounds appeared in his torso, but he ignored them.

A Dragon Soldier swung his bright silver spear like a scythe to take the imposter's head off. The blade struck his neck, but instead of decapitating him, the spear reacted as if it had struck something impossibly hard, and the shaft shook so violently the soldier lost his grip on it and it clattered to the ground.

The Protean stepped onto the platform, gave Lao Ran Jun one last infuriated glare, then disappeared.

Silence descended over the chamber. Dragon Soldiers moved to help their fallen. Those still in fighting shape took up positions around Lao Ran Jun.

One of his lieutenants who had witnessed the battle said in shock, "Lord General? What was that?"

"A shapshifter. A Jinin."

The lieutenant seemed even more rattled now. "A creature from legend?"

"Not legend," the Old Man said. "But a people with technology we lack. Initiate condition *baijiu*, Lieutenant."

"Condition *baijiu*," the soldier repeated. "Yes Lord General." He did not betray his surprise at the command to place the entire city under martial law and around-the-clock curfew.

Lao Ran Jun did not betray his own sense of dismay and doubt. How did one fight an indestructible creature, or find one who could take the shape of any person?

Catena 2

A brief flash of blue-white light struck me with vertigo. The disorientation was worse this time. Consecutive *peregrinations* screwed with the nervous system like jolts of electricity.

Before I could regain my balance, something struck me with a snarl and a cloud of hot, fetid breath, throwing me to my back and knocking the air out of me. I froze as a barbed spear blade glinted before my face.

A trio of Shen Dog Soldiers crouched around me. And standing over me, bearing the spear, stood one of the giant Dragon Soldiers clad in scarlet lamellar armor.

The tall soldier shouted at me, but I didn't understand. I held my hands out to show I posed no threat. "Take me to Lao Ran Jun." The guard continued to badger me with questions and what sounded like scolding, but I just kept repeating my request. Frustrated, the soldier motioned for me to rise.

I climbed to my feet, and the Dog Soldiers tensed, ready to spring on me. They were human, but they crouched on the balls of their feet. They wore simple loincloths. Their limbs were unusually long and muscular and their hands sported powerful, clawed hands. They growled, showing sharp fangs.

And now I had a better perspective and I gazed up at the giant in amazement. The man had to be almost three full meters tall, with a lithe, powerful torso and arms, pale skin, and bright, glittering eyes.

The Dragon Soldier gestured with his spear and I moved down the corridor and into the caverns. Alien purple trees sporting bioluminescent fruit filled the caverns with a pale light that cast multiple jagged shadows in every direction. The natural stone columns had been shaped into flying buttresses supporting upper tiers of walkways and chambers.

An eerie sound reached my ears. A young woman clad in plum and gold silk robes was singing in a thin, reedy voice a simple melody in a haunting pentatonic scale. She met my gaze and watched me pass while never faltering in her song.

I was led to an opulent chamber with scarlet, gold, and purple silk draping the natural stone walls. Before I could register the people in the room, one of them charged me.

Red-haired Tamara crashed into me and began to kiss me desperately, folding her body into me as if it were her natural state. The surprise and relief at seeing her, and the pleasure of it, had the best of me for a moment as I held her, returned her kisses, and breathed in her piquant scent.

"I love you," she whispered between kisses.

"I love you," I responded, reveling in her taste.

Then I realized Julian was there, watching. I pushed Tamara to the side, drew my gun and aimed it. Julian cocked my brow in amusement.

The white-haired, white-bearded old man with Julian made a subtle gesture and the giant guards at the door checked their moves toward me.

"Danny, no!" Tamara said.

"Is this how you greet me, Brother?" Julian said, his lips twitching in amusement.

"Fuck," I muttered. My instinct screamed at me to pull the trigger, but Tamara's presence confused me, and reminded me that the others remained in motion beyond my awareness. "Where are the other girls?"

"We don't know," Tamara said. "They were attacked."

I frowned at Julian.

"Not by me!" Julian said. "We have a new enemy. One dangerous enough to make our current spat seem petty."

"The pettiness of murdering your parents and siblings?" I asked.

Julian rewarded me with an annoyed glare.

Lao Ran Jun said, "You know this man?"

"He is Danny Nolan," Tamara said. "My husband."

Lao Ran Jun bowed. "Then greetings, Lord Danny. Our ancestors rejoice at our encounter."

I stifled my impulse to bow in return.

The old man spoke in my native language and one of the giant guards stepped to my side and drew a gold dagger.

"What the hell?" I said, pulling away.

"I vouch for him, Lord General," Tamara said, trying to interpose herself between me and the soldier.

"Nevertheless," said the old man.

"Do not resist this, Danny," said Julian. "The pain you experience will please me."

"Danny," Tamara said, taking my face in her hands and forcing me to gaze into her dark eyes. "Relax. Don't fight it. It will be over soon."

The guard took my left hand and slashed the dagger across my palm. There was a moment of no hurt, then stinging pain spread like acid through my hand and arm. The guard was not finished though. He thrust the tip of the blade into the bleeding wound and cut into one of the metacarpal muscles and then into the bone itself.

I gasped as deep, nauseating pain filled me, and I grunted, stifling the impulse to cry out. I continued to regard Tamara as I felt the blood drain from my face.

"I'm sorry," she said. "The girls were attacked by... something. We think it was a Protean. He looked human but he could change his appearance at will. And his body seemed impervious to injury."

The guard sheathed his gold dagger and took a scarlet cloth and used it to bind the wound respectfully. I clenched my fingers over the cloth, and pain throbbed to the pulse of my heartbeat.

"What," I said hoarsely. "Is a Protean?"

"Characters from legend," Tamara said. "Human brains and nervous systems joined with an artificial body. Hundreds of years ago, before medical technology had advanced enough to promise the longevity we have now, these artificial bodies were built to give virtual immortality to human consciousness."

"Cyborgs," I said, for a moment forgetting my pain and resentment in my amazement. "I'll be damned. But shape changing?"

"Probably a capacity of the carbynan material used to make the bodies. An early nanotechnology capable of changing its shape and appearance according to the needs of its host.

I thought about that. A race of shape-changing, impervious cyborgs could infiltrate any nation, any government. Any group. I glowered at Julian, who returned my glare and showed a red cloth wrapped around his own hand. I saw Tamara's left hand sported the same cloth. I took her hand in mine and kissed her bare knuckles.

"Are you okay, hon?"

She nodded.

"Then why are you still with him?" I said, nodding toward Julian.

She gave me a fleeting expression I could not decipher, a subtle look of appeal. Clearly, she did not want me to shoot Julian. At least, not yet. "We have reached an agreement with Lao Ran Jun. These Proteans threaten to destroy my people and he needs our help."

The old man stepped forward in his sharp uniform and bowed somberly. The aristocratic nature of his bearing, the serenity of his mien reminded me of old images of Robert E. Lee.

"Greetings, Danny Nolan," the old man said in flawless English. "Our ancestors smile upon our meeting. I and my family welcome you and your family in peace and honor." Even using simple English his inflections told me he promised no violence or harm to his visitors.

How much does he know about the Family? I asked Tamara.

More than he admits, she answered. *But not everything. Do not trust him.* This was a strange thing to hear, since Lao Ran Jun radiated tranquil trustworthiness like warm sunlight. *And use his full name.*

"Thank you for your generous greeting, Lao Ran Jun," said I, bowing in return, hoping I had the nuances right. "Your reputation as a superlative general and politician has reached even me, the least of your admirers. I am honored."

Wow. There was an amused twinkle in Tamara's eye.

"Danny is from the twenty-first century," Julian said, which gave the Lord General his first start of real surprise.

"2014," I said. "I was born in 1986."

Lao Ran Jun said, "Then I am doubly honored to meet the man who is both the oldest and the youngest of the *jiandie wang*." Time spies, my *ai* translated for me.

I thought the moment was over, but the old man continued to gaze at me. Now, however, his eyes had a distant cast to them, and he seemed to be preoccupied with something well beyond this chamber. Then he recollected himself with a visible blink and pursing of his lips. I realized Julian had been watching the old man with a faint smile.

There it was. Julian had promised Lao Ran Jun something; something available to a time-traveler. Something he yearned for. I don't know what it was, but Julian's expression of smug authority told me all I needed to know about his intentions. I raised my flechette gun to shoot Julian.

Something struck my arm hard and the gun clattered to the floor. A second blow caught me under the chin and I staggered. Tamara's arms caught me as my weight bore her to the ground. My ears rang from the impact, and for a moment I thought I was seeing double.

A second Julian Beran stood there, the one who had stopped me from killing the first. Yes, having an *analogue* did help, didn't it?

Lao Ran Jun stared at both Julians, and his Dragon Soldiers brought their spears to the ready.

The newly arrived Julian wore clothes of black and grey but appeared otherwise identical to the first. But he glared at me with naked fury.

"Meddling dupe!" he snapped. "I will make you grovel for absolution!" He held something in his hand, a small toroidal device that glittered in the light of the cavern.

Tamara appeared behind Julian even before I felt her absence behind me. She swung something, a curved handle that seemed to weigh a ton. With a spray of blood Julian's arm fell to the floor. The device in his hand struck the ground with an impact that I could feel through the rock. It did not bounce. Instead it punched a small crater in the natural stone, which radiated tiny cracks in all directions from it. The impact kicked up a cloud of dust.

Julian whirled on Tamara with an expression of incredulity, and disappeared, returning an instant later whole and furious. Tamara sensed his return and whirled. She discarded the cumbersome labrys and began to rain blows on Julian.

I scrambled for my gun, but the first Julian kicked me in the face. Even as my blood sprayed around me, I sank my conscious thought into my *ai* and triggered the failsafe. I *peregrinated* behind the Julian *analogue* just as he kicked out. The blood sprayed, and the version of myself on the ground disappeared with a blue-white flash, and I swept Julian's leg out from under him.

I dove past him to the gun and rolled into a crouch, taking aim at the dark-clad Julian facing Tamara. I pulled the trigger, but somehow Julian moved faster, grabbing Tamara's arms and pulling her into the line of fire. Three flechette wounds appeared in her shoulder as Julian flung her at me.

I froze in horror, catching her even as I realized my Alphan-modified weapon was going to kill the woman I loved. Her expression was shocked and blanched from the pain.

I forgot about everything else. No! I was about to activate my failsafe again, to stop myself from shooting her, but a heavy blow on my neck knocked me across her body.

"I claim that for myself," Julian said from somewhere behind me.

"A potent weapon, if it was able to draw this revelation from you," said Lao Ran Jun.

"Yes. Someone modified it for me."

"Who?"

"I don't know. But I will find out."

A violent electric shock tore through I and I cried out, and beneath me Tamara sobbed.

Deadened senses registered in me as I was picked up and hurled against the stone wall. My impact ripped a blue silk hanging from its hooks and it fluttered down to cover me.

Julian, the one in black, tore the silk from my form. He had recovered his toroidal device and pointed it at me. My modified flechette gun he had thrust into his belt.

"Who?" Julian said.

"Perhaps he modified it himself," said Lao Ran Jun.

Julian gave a short, contemptuous laugh. "He is an ape. An unevolved primate barely removed from picking lice from his fur to eat." His lips twisted as me regarded me. "Who helped you?" He pointed the device at Tamara. An inky blackness--shot through with rippling sparks--leapt from it, and she screamed as she convulsed. The wound in her shoulder grew darker with each passing moment as black blood saturated her shirt and smeared the floor beneath her.

"No!" I tried to shout. It came out as the barest, hoarse whisper. "No..."

"Speak!" Julian snapped. "She dies, but not quickly. I can bring her misery to a climax. She will die screaming unless you speak."

"Help me... save her!" I whispered. "Please. We both love her."

Julian gave the slightest of flinches, so minor that I might have mistaken it for scorn.

"She's your sister!" I said. I searched inside myself for my *ai*, but whatever Julian had shot me with had left it disrupted.

"And your beloved!" Julian retorted. "And you are the one who has slain her. Think on that, Ape!"

"Please," I said, and tears rolled down my face. "I will do what you want. Just save her."

Julian smiled. "Wisdom comes at last!"

"The Alphans," I said. "They changed the gun to fill the darts with nanites."

Julian's expression changed to startled apprehension. His eyes flicked around as if a new threat had materialized in the chamber. "The Alphans..." He swallowed. He exchanged glances with his *analogue*. Both were rattled by the information. And now I knew who Julian truly feared. "Do it."

The *analogue* Julian nodded sharply and disappeared.

Abruptly, the shape of the cavern changed and darkened. The natural bioluminescence took on a violet and ultraviolet hue. All the human touches, the silks, the tables, chairs, and rugs, and the oxygen, were gone as if they never existed. A misty gas filled the cavern, and those who breathed it coughed and gagged. And all the Shen were gone. Only Lao Ran Jun remained, gasping and coughing in the alien atmosphere.

The black clad Julian drew the Alphan-modified weapon. "I knew I would have to act against them eventually. Their prowess would have been superlative joined with mine. But they lack ambition. They could conquer the known universe if they decided to. So, in the end, they are just sentient abaci." His words dripped with derision. "Tools. No better than any other tools." He aimed at me.

252

"Julian."

A new voice sounded, a woman's voice. Julian caught his breath.

A woman I had never seen stood there, between me and Julian. She was slim, angular, and had long, straight blonde hair. Her resemblance to Alea told me who she had to be. Next to her stood dark-haired, *analogue* Tamara.

"*Mazhea*," Julian said, appearing abruptly too young and vulnerable. Mother.

Sheyn Liann, the only one of the Family to die, who took her own life when she realized she was an *analogue* rather than break the most important tenet of the Family's purpose.

"Please, Julian," she said. "Do not do this. We can fix this."

Julian shook his head. "You're dead." He blinked as if he did not believe his own eyes.

Sheyn smiled. "Death is… illusory to those who have mastered Time."

Julian's eyes narrowed. "You're an *analogue*."

She said, "I am your mother. I bore you, named you, and loved you first, before all others knew you. Before you even knew yourself I knew you, and held you, and cherished you." She held her hands to me in supplication. She coughed in the putrid atmosphere that filled the cavern.

"Please, Julian," she gasped. "I bring a message from the Elders. We agree with you now. We chose the wrong path, the path of self-sacrifice. You were right to despise us for it. You, Paul, and the other children were right to demand more, to take a more active role in the struggles of our race. I speak for all the Elders and for all the Children. I speak for the Family when I tell you were right, Julian. The rebellion is over. You have won. There is no more need for violence."

Julian stared at her, and conflict raged across his face. His hand wavered, then steadied. He continued to aim at me, and thus through his mother.

Bitter anger narrowed his eyes. "I had one mother, and she is dead. You are a parlor trick meant to deceive me." His aim steadied.

"Julian," she said. Now her voice was stern, scolding. "To shoot him you have to shoot me. If you care not about killing me then you are truly lost to me. But know this young man: *you will not kill me*!"

The tone of her voice made him hesitate.

"I say that," Sheyn said. "Not because I command you. But because I am warning you. The Alphans changed the gun. It was designed to kill you. *You*. What do you think will happen when it detects *you* pulling the trigger?"

But her warning went unheeded. An expression of incredulity filled Julian's face. "You knew! You've known about all of this. You've been working with the Ape! You betrayed me from the start!"

"I know because the Alphans told me before sending me here!" Sheyn snapped. "They mean to destroy you, and have multiple actions in play. But I am betraying them, not you. Flee, my son. Get away from here. I love you and I can't see you hurt. Go!" She put the full force of her maternal fervor into the command.

Doubt flickered in Julian's eyes. Then he pressed his lips together and pulled the trigger.

Blackness erupted from the silver weapon and consumed it in the blink of an eye, along with Julian's hand and arm. He gaped at the black substance that flowed up his arm and into his shoulder. He began to scream in agony and panic. He dropped his toroid, and it again slammed into the floor and left a small crater in the stone.

Julian tried to bat at the substance with his free hand, but that only spread it more quickly. It covered and saturated his torso and then his head, finally, mercifully, cutting off his screams.

In the silence, Sheyn slid to her knees, covered her face with her hands, and wept.

I crawled over to Tamara, beautiful Tamara who had opened my eyes to this amazing, and horrifying, future. But her eyes were closed.

I groaned even as I gasped for breath. No! There was something. There had to be something. But no. The Alphans had designed it to kill, and it had killed efficiently.

Tamara, the real Tamara, who I had helped from the hospital, who had told me the truth before I was ready to accept it, who had fallen into her mad brother's clutches before redeeming herself, was gone. As was the man who had taken and broken her.

I felt cold, gentle hands on my shoulders. The *analogue* Tamara wrapped her arms around me and held me as I sobbed.

Epilogue

"Done," Lor said with an air of self-congratulation. The *sirdar* flickered and hummed faintly as it returned to life.

"Now we wait and see what it finds," said Kyren, sitting next to him watching a display in the air over the table. I stood behind them, and next to me stood Sheyn Liann.

The master computer queried the metadata it had *peregrinated* to different times and locations, and retrieved them to compare them to its current repository. It could not detect actual changes to the timeline as they occurred. It could only compare what it knew now to what it had known yesterday.

The display started flickering as data began to flow across it. A large amount of the data was formatted in bright, glowing red letters, indicating changes.

"Damn," Sheyn muttered. "Damn damn damn!"

"What does it say?" I asked. I was not yet fluent enough in the alphabet of this century to read it without the help of my *ai*, which was excessively slow.

"Well, it confirms your reconnaissance to your time of origin, Danny," said Kyren. "Julian has rewritten history."

When I had returned to my original time, I'd stayed only long enough to verify that Earth had changed drastically. Julian had somehow prevented the eruption of Thera that had destroyed the advanced Minoan civilization on Crete, and then used his foreknowledge and abilities to take control and make the civilization flourish.

It disconcerted me that as of now, I was the last human being to learn of Greece, and Rome, Alexander the Great, and the great dynasties of Egypt and China. All now were mere side notes, subsumed by the Minoans, who had experienced the Enlightenment, the Industrial Age, and then the Space Age four thousand years earlier.

Lor and Kyren read the images, committing them to their *ai*-enhanced memories. Then the four of them returned to their new base of operations, a cave in what had, in another timeline, been known as Australia.

The rest of the Family was waiting for them in the conference room, including the only person who, perhaps, was more disconcerted by the turn of events than I was. Lao Ran Jun, the Lord General of a people that now had never existed. His ability to *peregrinate* had rendered him immune to the erasure of the Shen but now he was alone in the universe. His capabilities made it easy for the Elders to make him a de facto member of the Family. But he seemed ill-at-ease in the casual environment.

I strode to Tamara. She smiled up at me and accepted my kiss as I sat next to her. I took her hand. Her fingers were ice cold, and I began to rub some warmth back into them. I stole a glance at her, dark hair framing a brown face of breathtaking beauty. She rarely smiled anymore. She tended to wear a perpetually troubled expression that haunted me. I understood. Or thought I did.

I had tried repeatedly to explain that I loved her, Tamara Decaire, even if there had been two of her. I loved them equally because to me they were the same. I knew it would take time. This Tamara was tortured by a sense of inadequacy she might never overcome. Even though she had been the one to find and retrieve Sheyn, convince her to return, and seek the help of the Alphans. Without this Tamara, Julian's plans would have come to fruition, and he would have ruled the present as well as the past. I squeezed her hand reassuringly and she smiled at me.

Together, Lor and Kyren briefed the rest about Julian's changes. The biggest, and thus the focus for any attempt to reverse Julian, was the eruption of the Thera volcano.

"Can we set it off?" Yana Cartine asked.

Arran Decaire nodded. "No doubt whatsoever."

"Julian knows we will pick that nexus," Tamara said. Then she flushed and looked down at the polished table.

"Yes," Paul said. "Which is why we'll need a distraction."

"And," Arran said, cocking a white brow at the younger man, "All the intelligence we can get."

"And start well ahead of the planned event," Kyren said. "The way I did with the Shen." She smiled and winked at Lao Ran Jun, who nodded.

The old man said, "Lady Kyren is correct. I knew to expect three women fleeing Julian's attack. When only two arrived, I was suspicious. But I never suspected Li Lin Zha, whom I had known for years before even learning of your Family."

Arran nodded. "We will send three teams. Myself and Sheyn, Paul and Tamara, and Danny and Alea. And Kyren will do what she does best."

The younger generation exchanged glances at that.

"I work alone," Paul said.

"As do I," Tamara said, but with much less assertion.

I wanted to protest, because I had been looking forward to working with Tamara in the field.

"And you will," said Arran. "Just set up a regular method to check up on each other."

"And I will be at the proxy site if you need me," said Yana.

Lao Ran Jun stirred and looked at Yana and Reys Andresen. "Have you found a way to expose any Proteans they may encounter?"

"Almost," said Reys. "We want something that can detect the artificial material without tipping off the target. We are using a phased *Kaph* field because we believe the Proteans are not as proficient as we are in dynamic field technology. Now it's just a matter of reprogramming our nanites to detect it. The injections should be ready in a few days at the proxy site." Yana nodded at that.

"It's also possible," Sheyn said, "That Julian erased the Proteans the way he did the Shen and the Alphans."

"For which we should be grateful," Paul muttered. Then he coughed. "No offense, Lord General."

The old man nodded mildly.

Tamara gave me an amused glance, which I returned with a grin.

"Anything else?" Arran said. "Very well, we are adjourned. Relax, and prepare. Yana will start the injections to change our outward appearances to blend in with the Bronze Age Minoans. Not as efficient at shapechanging as the Proteans, but good enough."

***

Tamara walked down to the crypt, even though no bodies were kept there.

There were only cubes displaying moving images of the people they had lost:

Herol Beran, the mastermind who had created the Family and foreseen this crisis, but had not survived it.

Lerys Eril, her beloved uncle who had given her the idea to find Sheyn, and who had gone on to face death at the hands of Tamara Prime knowing ahead of time it was his fate.

Sheyn Liann, the oldest of the memorials. The new *analogue* Sheyn had accepted her place and rejoined the Family, but no one knew what to do with this cenotaph.

Finally, a place for the last, unfinished memorial, to Tamara Decaire. Like Sheyn's, this one was in limbo as people struggled with the confusion of the analogues.

Tamara chuckled to herself. Add a word to the dictionary. Like a gaggle of geese, or a murder of crows, she proposed a confusion of analogues.

Sheyn had helped her a great deal, actually. Likewise, Tamara had helped her with the situation. Together they were sharing their doubts, and their sense that they had no place in this world, and their efforts to come to terms with the reality.

But Tamara had not confided in Sheyn her conviction that the real Tamara had died in this fight. She had not told Sheyn of the dark despair that beat on the edges of her spirit and sought to consume her. Tamara didn't know who she was, but she never revealed to Sheyn her belief that she didn't deserve a place with these people; nor the clear necessity for her to end her existence after the Family repaired Julian's damage to the timeline.

She heard light steps behind her. Danny wrapped his warm arms around her and she leaned into him, holding his strong hands. He had become her rock, her guiding star, and she had been lost when she thought she'd lost him.

Now she had found him again, and his strength and love had kept her despair at bay. The doubts remained, as did the lure of a final darkness, but he kept her anchored. She had a duty to the Family and to humanity to see Julian defeated and the natural *catenae* restored.

After that? Well. If the black hole still beckoned, she would see. But for now they were together. She drew in the sensations of Danny's reassuring presence, his warmth, his musky scent, his strength, and they rocked gently together in front of Tamara's unfinished memorial.

THE END

www.ingramcontent.com/pod-product-compliance
Lightning Source LLC
Chambersburg PA
CBHW050459260626
47157CB00004B/1112